ENGLISH BARDS AND SCOTCH REVIEWERS: A SATIRE
BY
Lord Byron

ENGLISH BARDS AND SCOTCH REVIEWERS: A SATIRE

Published by Krill Press

New York City, NY

First published 1809

Copyright © Krill Press, 2015

All rights reserved

Except in the United States of America, this book is sold subject to the condition that it shall not, by way of trade or otherwise, be lent, re-sold, hired out, or otherwise circulated without the publisher's prior consent in any form of binding or cover other than that in which it is published and without a similar condition including this condition being imposed on the subsequent purchaser.

ABOUT KRILL PRESS

Krill Press is a boutique publishing company run by people who are passionate about history's greatest works. We strive to republish the best books ever written across every conceivable genre and making them easily and cheaply available to readers across the world. Please visit our site for more information.

Introduction

At a time when the Romantic movement was sweeping the European continent in the early 19th century, among musicians, writers and playwrights, perhaps nobody embodied and personified the Romantic movement quite like **Lord Byron**, the famous English poet whose life and works are both the stuff of legend.

In addition to being celebrated for poems like *She Walks in Beauty*, *When We Two Parted*, and *So, we'll go no more a roving*, Byron was also notorious for living in excess, racking up debts and liaisons at increasingly reckless speeds. Despite his fame and abilities, he eventually exiled himself, ultimately traveling to fight in the Greek War of Independence against the Ottoman Turks. Lord Byron would fall ill and die during the war at the young age of 36, but the Greeks consider him a national hero, and people have been reading his material and talking about his life ever since.

English Bards and Scotch Reviewers; A Satire
BY
LORD BYRON.

"I had rather be a kitten, and cry, mew!
Than one of these same metre ballad-mongers."

SHAKESPEARE.

"Such shameless Bards we have; and yet 'tis true,
There are as mad, abandon'd Critics, too."

POPE.

PREFACE [1]

All my friends, learned and unlearned, have urged me not to publish this Satire with my name. If I were to be "turned from the career of my humour by quibbles quick, and paper bullets of the brain" I should have complied with their counsel. But I am not to be terrified by abuse, or bullied by reviewers, with or without arms. I can safely say that I have attacked none 'personally', who did not commence on the offensive. An Author's works are public property: he who purchases may judge, and publish his opinion if he pleases; and the Authors I have endeavoured to commemorate may do by me as I have done by them. I dare say they will succeed better in condemning my scribblings, than in mending their own. But my object is not to prove that I can write well, but, if 'possible', to make others write better.

As the Poem has met with far more success than I expected, I have endeavoured in this Edition to make some additions and alterations, to render it more worthy of public perusal.

In the First Edition of this Satire, published anonymously, fourteen lines on the subject of Bowles's Pope were written by, and inserted at the request of, an ingenious friend of mine, [2] who has now in the press a volume of Poetry. In the present Edition they are erased, and some of my own substituted in their stead; my only reason for this being that which I conceive would operate with any other person in the same manner,—a determination not to publish with my name any production, which was not entirely and exclusively my own composition.

With [3] regard to the real talents of many of the poetical persons whose performances are mentioned or alluded to in the following pages, it is presumed by the Author that there can be little difference of opinion in the Public at large; though, like other sectaries, each has his separate tabernacle of proselytes, by whom his abilities are over-rated, his faults overlooked, and his metrical canons received without scruple and without consideration. But the unquestionable possession of considerable genius by several of the writers here censured renders their mental prostitution more to be regretted. Imbecility may be pitied, or, at worst, laughed at and forgotten; perverted powers demand the most decided reprehension. No one can wish more than the Author that some known and able writer had undertaken their exposure; but Mr. Gifford has devoted himself to Massinger, and, in the absence of the regular physician, a country practitioner may, in cases of absolute necessity, be allowed to prescribe his nostrum to prevent the extension of so deplorable an epidemic, provided there be no quackery in his treatment of the malady. A caustic is here offered; as it is to be feared nothing short of actual cautery can recover the numerous patients afflicted with the present prevalent and distressing rabies for rhyming.—As to the 'Edinburgh Reviewers', it would indeed require an Hercules to crush the Hydra; but if the Author succeeds in merely "bruising one of the heads of the serpent" though his own hand should suffer in the encounter, he will be amply satisfied.

[Footnote 1: The Preface, as it is here printed, was prefixed to the Second, Third, and Fourth Editions of 'English Bards, and Scotch Reviewers'. The preface to the First Edition began with the words, "With regard to the real talents," etc. The text of the poem follows that of the suppressed Fifth Edition, which passed under Byron's own supervision, and was to have been issued in 1812. From that Edition the Preface was altogether excluded.

In an annotated copy of the Fourth Edition, of 1811, underneath the note, "This preface was written for the Second Edition, and printed with it. The noble author had left this country previous to the publication of that Edition, and is not yet returned," Byron wrote, in 1816, "He is, and gone again."—MS. Notes from this volume, which is now in Mr. Murray's possession, are marked—B., 1816.]

[Footnote 2: John Cam Hobhouse.]

[Footnote 3: Preface to the First Edition.]

INTRODUCTION TO ENGLISH BARDS, AND SCOTCH REVIEWERS.

The article upon 'Hours of Idleness' "which Lord Brougham ... after denying it for thirty years, confessed that he had written" ('Notes from a Diary', by Sir M. E. Grant Duff, 1897, ii. 189), was published in the 'Edinburgh Review' of January, 1808. 'English Bards, and Scotch Reviewers' did not appear till March, 1809. The article gave the opportunity for the publication of the satire, but only in part provoked its composition. Years later, Byron had not forgotten its effect on his mind. On April 26, 1821, he wrote to Shelley: "I recollect the effect on me of the Edinburgh on my first poem: it was rage and resistance and redress: but not despondency nor despair." And on the same date to Murray: "I know by experience that a savage review is hemlock to a sucking author; and the one on me (which produced the 'English Bards', etc.) knocked me down, but I got up again," etc. It must, however, be remembered that Byron had his weapons ready for an attack before he used them in defence. In a letter to Miss Pigot, dated October 26, 1807, he says that "he has written one poem of 380 lines to be published in a few weeks with notes. The poem ... is a Satire." It was entitled 'British Bards', and finally numbered 520 lines. With a view to publication, or for his own convenience, it was put up in type and printed in quarto sheets. A single copy, which he kept for corrections and additions, was preserved by Dallas, and is now in the British Museum. After the review appeared, he enlarged and recast the 'British Bards', and in March, 1809, the Satire was published anonymously. Byron was at no pains to conceal the authorship of 'English Bards, and Scotch Reviewers', and, before starting on his Pilgrimage, he had prepared a second and enlarged edition, which came out in October, 1809, with his name prefixed. Two more editions were called for in his absence, and on his return he revised and printed a fifth, when he suddenly resolved to suppress the work. On his homeward voyage he expressed, in a letter to Dallas, June 28, 1811, his regret at having written the Satire. A year later he became intimate, among others, with Lord and Lady Holland, whom he had assailed on the supposition that they were the instigators of the article in the 'Edinburgh Review', and on being told by Rogers that they wished the Satire to be withdrawn, he gave orders to his publisher, Cawthorn, to burn the whole impression. A few copies escaped the flames. One of two copies retained by Dallas, which afterwards belonged to Murray, and is now in his grandson's possession, was the foundation of the text of 1831, and of all subsequent issues. Another copy which belonged to Dallas is retained in the British Museum.

Towards the close of the last century there had been an outburst of satirical poems, written in the style of the 'Dunciad' and its offspring the 'Rosciad', Of these, Gifford's 'Baviad' and 'Maviad' (1794-5), and T. J. Mathias' 'Pursuits of Literature' (1794-7), were the direct progenitors of 'English Bards, and Scotch Reviewers', The 'Rolliad' (1794), the 'Children of Apollo' (circ. 1794), Canning's 'New Morality' (1798), and Wolcot's coarse but virile lampoons, must also be reckoned among Byron's earlier models. The ministry of "All the Talents" gave rise to a fresh batch of political 'jeux d'ésprits', and in 1807, when Byron was still at Cambridge, the air was full of these ephemera. To name only a few, 'All the Talents', by Polypus (Eaton Stannard Barrett), was answered by 'All the Blocks, an antidote to All the Talents', by Flagellum (W. H. Ireland); 'Elijah's Mantle, a tribute to the memory of the R. H. William Pitt', by James Sayer, the caricaturist, provoked 'Melville's Mantle, being a Parody on ... Elijah's Mantle'. 'The Simpliciad, A Satirico-Didactic Poem', and Lady Anne Hamilton's 'Epics of the Ton', are also of the same period. One and all have perished, but Byron read them, and in a greater or less degree they supplied the impulse to write in the fashion of the day.

'British Bards' would have lived, but, unquestionably, the spur of the article, a year's delay, and, above all, the advice and criticism of his friend Hodgson, who was at work on his 'Gentle Alterative for the Reviewers', 1809 (for further details, see vol. i., 'Letters', Letter 102, 'note' 1), produced the brilliant success of the enlarged satire. 'English Bards, and Scotch Reviewers' was recognized at once as a work of genius. It has intercepted the popularity of its great predecessors, who are often quoted, but seldom read. It is still a popular poem, and appeals with fresh delight to readers who know the names of many of the "bards" only because Byron mentions them, and count others whom he ridicules among the greatest poets of the century.

ENGLISH BARDS AND SCOTCH REVIEWERS. [1]

    Still [2] must I hear?—shall hoarse [3] FITZGERALD bawl
His creaking couplets in a tavern hall,
And I not sing, lest, haply, Scotch Reviews
Should dub me scribbler, and denounce my *Muse?*
Prepare for rhyme—I'll publish, right or wrong:
Fools are my theme, let Satire be my song. [i]

    Oh! Nature's noblest gift—my grey goose-quill!
Slave of my thoughts, obedient to my will,
Torn from thy parent bird to form a pen,
That mighty instrument of little men!   10
The pen! foredoomed to aid the mental throes
Of brains that labour, big with Verse or Prose;
Though Nymphs forsake, and Critics may deride,
The Lover's solace, and the Author's pride.
What Wits! what Poets dost thou daily raise!
How frequent is thy use, how small thy praise!
Condemned at length to be forgotten quite,
With all the pages which 'twas thine to write.
But thou, at least, mine own especial pen! [ii]
Once laid aside, but now assumed again,   20
Our task complete, like Hamet's [4] shall be free;
Though spurned by others, yet beloved by me:
Then let us soar to-day; no common theme,
No Eastern vision, no distempered dream [5]
Inspires—our path, though full of thorns, is plain;
Smooth be the verse, and easy be the strain.

    When Vice triumphant holds her sov'reign sway,
Obey'd by all who nought beside obey; [iii]
When Folly, frequent harbinger of crime,
Bedecks her cap with bells of every Clime; [iv]   30
When knaves and fools combined o'er all prevail,
And weigh their Justice in a Golden Scale; [v]

E'en then the boldest start from public sneers,
Afraid of Shame, unknown to other fears,
More darkly sin, by Satire kept in awe,
And shrink from Ridicule, though not from Law.

   Such is the force of Wit! I but not belong
To me the arrows of satiric song;
The royal vices of our age demand
A keener weapon, and a mightier hand. [vi]   40
Still there are follies, e'en for me to chase,
And yield at least amusement in the race:
Laugh when I laugh, I seek no other fame,
The cry is up, and scribblers are my game:
Speed, Pegasus!—ye strains of great and small,
Ode! Epic! Elegy!—have at you all!
I, too, can scrawl, and once upon a time
I poured along the town a flood of rhyme,
A schoolboy freak, unworthy praise or blame;
I printed—older children do the same.   50
'Tis pleasant, sure, to see one's name in print;
A Book's a Book, altho' there's nothing in't.
Not that a Title's sounding charm can save [vii]
Or scrawl or scribbler from an equal grave:
This LAMB [6] must own, since his patrician name
Failed to preserve the spurious Farce from shame. [7]
No matter, GEORGE continues still to write, [8]
Tho' now the name is veiled from public sight.
Moved by the great example, I pursue
The self-same road, but make my own review: 60
Not seek great JEFFREY'S, yet like him will be
Self-constituted Judge of Poesy.

   A man must serve his time to every trade
Save Censure—Critics all are ready made.
Take hackneyed jokes from MILLER, [9] got by rote,
With just enough of learning to misquote;
A man well skilled to find, or forge a fault;
A turn for punning—call it Attic salt;
To JEFFREY go, be silent and discreet,
His pay is just ten sterling pounds per sheet: 70
Fear not to lie,'twill seem a *sharper* hit; [viii]

Shrink not from blasphemy, 'twill pass for wit;
Care not for feeling—pass your proper jest,
And stand a Critic, hated yet caress'd.

  And shall we own such judgment? no—as soon
Seek roses in December—ice in June;
Hope constancy in wind, or corn in chaff,
Believe a woman or an epitaph,
Or any other thing that's false, before
You trust in Critics, who themselves are sore;   80
Or yield one single thought to be misled
By JEFFREY'S heart, or LAMB'S Boeotian head. [10]
To these young tyrants, by themselves misplaced,
Combined usurpers on the Throne of Taste;
To these, when Authors bend in humble awe,
And hail their voice as Truth, their word as Law;
While these are Censors, 'twould be sin to spare; [11]
While such are Critics, why should I forbear?
But yet, so near all modern worthies run,
'Tis doubtful whom to seek, or whom to shun;   90
Nor know we when to spare, or where to strike,
Our Bards and Censors are so much alike.
Then should you ask me, [12] why I venture o'er
The path which POPE and GIFFORD [13] trod before;
If not yet sickened, you can still proceed;
Go on; my rhyme will tell you as you read.
"But hold!" exclaims a friend,—"here's some neglect:
This—that—and t'other line seem incorrect."
What then? the self-same blunder Pope has got,
And careless Dryden—"Aye, but Pye has not:"—   100
Indeed!—'tis granted, faith!—but what care I?
Better to err with POPE, than shine with PYE. [14]

  Time was, ere yet in these degenerate days [15]
Ignoble themes obtained mistaken praise,
When Sense and Wit with Poesy allied,
No fabled Graces, flourished side by side,
From the same fount their inspiration drew,
And, reared by Taste, bloomed fairer as they grew.
Then, in this happy Isle, a POPE'S pure strain
Sought the rapt soul to charm, nor sought in vain;   110

A polished nation's praise aspired to claim,
And raised the people's, as the poet's fame.
Like him great DRYDEN poured the tide of song,
In stream less smooth, indeed, yet doubly strong.
Then CONGREVE'S scenes could cheer, or OTWAY'S melt; [16]
For Nature then an English audience felt—
But why these names, or greater still, retrace,
When all to feebler Bards resign their place?
Yet to such times our lingering looks are cast,
When taste and reason with those times are past.   120
Now look around, and turn each trifling page,
Survey the precious works that please the age;
This truth at least let Satire's self allow,
No dearth of Bards can be complained of now. [ix]
The loaded Press beneath her labour groans, [x]
And Printers' devils shake their weary bones;
While SOUTHEY'S Epics cram the creaking shelves, [xi]
And LITTLE'S Lyrics shine in hot-pressed twelves. [17]
Thus saith the *Preacher*: "Nought beneath the sun
Is new," [18] yet still from change to change we run.   130
What varied wonders tempt us as they pass!
The Cow-pox, Tractors, Galvanism, and Gas, [19]
In turns appear, to make the vulgar stare,
Till the swoln bubble bursts—and all is air!
Nor less new schools of Poetry arise,
Where dull pretenders grapple for the prize:
O'er Taste awhile these Pseudo-bards prevail; [xii]
Each country Book-club bows the knee to Baal,
And, hurling lawful Genius from the throne,
Erects a shrine and idol of its own; [xiii]   140
Some leaden calf—but whom it matters not,
From soaring SOUTHEY, down to groveling STOTT. [20]

   Behold! in various throngs the scribbling crew,
For notice eager, pass in long review:
Each spurs his jaded Pegasus apace,
And Rhyme and Blank maintain an equal race;
Sonnets on sonnets crowd, and ode on ode;
And Tales of Terror [21] jostle on the road;
Immeasurable measures move along;
For simpering Folly loves a varied song,   150

To strange, mysterious Dulness still the friend,
Admires the strain she cannot comprehend.
Thus Lays of Minstrels [22]—may they be the last!—
On half-strung harps whine mournful to the blast.
While mountain spirits prate to river sprites,
That dames may listen to the sound at nights;
And goblin brats, of Gilpin Horner's [23] brood
Decoy young Border-nobles through the wood,
And skip at every step, Lord knows how high,
And frighten foolish babes, the Lord knows why;   160
While high-born ladies in their magic cell,
Forbidding Knights to read who cannot spell,
Despatch a courier to a wizard's grave,
And fight with honest men to shield a knave.

   Next view in state, proud prancing on his roan,
The golden-crested haughty Marmion,
Now forging scrolls, now foremost in the fight,
Not quite a Felon, yet but half a Knight. [xiv]
The gibbet or the field prepared to grace;
A mighty mixture of the great and base.   170
And think'st thou, SCOTT! by vain conceit perchance,
On public taste to foist thy stale romance,
Though MURRAY with his MILLER may combine
To yield thy muse just half-a-crown per line? [24]
No! when the sons of song descend to trade,
Their bays are sear, their former laurels fade,
Let such forego the poet's sacred name,
Who rack their brains for lucre, not for fame:
Still for stern Mammon may they toil in vain! [25]
And sadly gaze on Gold they cannot gain!   180
Such be their meed, such still the just reward [xv]
Of prostituted Muse and hireling bard!
For this we spurn Apollo's venal son,
And bid a long "good night to Marmion." [26]

   These are the themes that claim our plaudits now;
These are the Bards to whom the Muse must bow;
While MILTON, DRYDEN, POPE, alike forgot,
Resign their hallowed Bays to WALTER SCOTT.

    The time has been, when yet the Muse was young,
When HOMER swept the lyre, and MARO sung,   190
An Epic scarce ten centuries could claim,
While awe-struck nations hailed the magic name:
The work of each immortal Bard appears
The single wonder of a thousand years. [27]
Empires have mouldered from the face of earth,
Tongues have expired with those who gave them birth,
Without the glory such a strain can give,
As even in ruin bids the language live.
Not so with us, though minor Bards, content, [xvi]
On one great work a life of labour spent: 200
With eagle pinion soaring to the skies,
Behold the Ballad-monger SOUTHEY rise!
To him let CAMOËNS, MILTON, TASSO yield,
Whose annual strains, like armies, take the field.
First in the ranks see Joan of Arc advance,
The scourge of England and the boast of France!
Though burnt by wicked BEDFORD for a witch,
Behold her statue placed in Glory's niche;
Her fetters burst, and just released from prison,
A virgin Phoenix from her ashes risen.   210
Next see tremendous Thalaba come on, [28]
Arabia's monstrous, wild, and wond'rous son;
Domdaniel's dread destroyer, who o'erthrew
More mad magicians than the world e'er knew.
Immortal Hero! all thy foes o'ercome,
For ever reign—the rival of Tom Thumb! [29]
Since startled Metre fled before thy face,
Well wert thou doomed the last of all thy race!
Well might triumphant Genii bear thee hence,
Illustrious conqueror of common sense!   220
Now, last and greatest, Madoc spreads his sails,
Cacique in Mexico, [30] and Prince in Wales;
Tells us strange tales, as other travellers do,
More old than Mandeville's, and not so true.
Oh, SOUTHEY! SOUTHEY! [31] cease thy varied song!
A bard may chaunt too often and too long:
As thou art strong in verse, in mercy, spare!
A fourth, alas! were more than we could bear.

But if, in spite of all the world can say,
Thou still wilt verseward plod thy weary way; 230
If still in Berkeley-Ballads most uncivil,
Thou wilt devote old women to the devil, [32]
The babe unborn thy dread intent may rue:
"God help thee," SOUTHEY, [33] and thy readers too.

   Next comes the dull disciple of thy school, [34]
That mild apostate from poetic rule,
The simple WORDSWORTH, framer of a lay
As soft as evening in his favourite May,
Who warns his friend "to shake off toil and trouble,
And quit his books, for fear of growing double;" [35] 240
Who, both by precept and example, shows
That prose is verse, and verse is merely prose;
Convincing all, by demonstration plain,
Poetic souls delight in prose insane;
And Christmas stories tortured into rhyme
Contain the essence of the true sublime.
Thus, when he tells the tale of Betty Foy,
The idiot mother of "an idiot Boy;"
A moon-struck, silly lad, who lost his way,
And, like his bard, confounded night with day [36] 250
So close on each pathetic part he dwells,
And each adventure so sublimely tells,
That all who view the "idiot in his glory"
Conceive the Bard the hero of the story.

   Shall gentle COLERIDGE pass unnoticed here, [37]
To turgid ode and tumid stanza dear?
Though themes of innocence amuse him best,
Yet still Obscurity's a welcome guest.
If Inspiration should her aid refuse
To him who takes a Pixy for a muse, [38] 260
Yet none in lofty numbers can surpass
The bard who soars to elegize an ass:
So well the subject suits his noble mind, [xvii]
He brays, the Laureate of the long-eared kind. [xviii]

   Oh! wonder-working LEWIS! [39] Monk, or Bard,
Who fain would make Parnassus a church-yard! [xix]

Lo! wreaths of yew, not laurel, bind thy brow,
Thy Muse a Sprite, Apollo's sexton thou!
Whether on ancient tombs thou tak'st thy stand,
By gibb'ring spectres hailed, thy kindred band;   270
Or tracest chaste descriptions on thy page,
To please the females of our modest age;
All hail, M.P.! [40] from whose infernal brain
Thin-sheeted phantoms glide, a grisly train;
At whose command "grim women" throng in crowds,
And kings of fire, of water, and of clouds,
With "small grey men,"—"wild yagers," and what not,
To crown with honour thee and WALTER SCOTT:
Again, all hail! if tales like thine may please,
St. Luke alone can vanquish the disease: 280
Even Satan's self with thee might dread to dwell,
And in thy skull discern a deeper Hell.

  Who in soft guise, surrounded by a choir
Of virgins melting, not to Vesta's fire,
With sparkling eyes, and cheek by passion flushed
Strikes his wild lyre, whilst listening dames are hushed?
'Tis LITTLE! young Catullus of his day,
As sweet, but as immoral, in his Lay!
Grieved to condemn, the Muse must still be just,
Nor spare melodious advocates of lust.   290
Pure is the flame which o'er her altar burns;
From grosser incense with disgust she turns
Yet kind to youth, this expiation o'er,
She bids thee "mend thy line, and sin no more." [xx]

  For thee, translator of the tinsel song,
To whom such glittering ornaments belong,
Hibernian STRANGFORD! with thine eyes of blue, [41]
And boasted locks of red or auburn hue,
Whose plaintive strain each love-sick Miss admires,
And o'er harmonious fustian half expires, [xxi]   300
Learn, if thou canst, to yield thine author's sense,
Nor vend thy sonnets on a false pretence.
Think'st thou to gain thy verse a higher place,
By dressing Camoëns [42] in a suit of lace?
Mend, STRANGFORD! mend thy morals and thy taste;

Be warm, but pure; be amorous, but be chaste:
Cease to deceive; thy pilfered harp restore,
Nor teach the Lusian Bard to copy MOORE.

  Behold—Ye Tarts!—one moment spare the text! [xxii]—
HAYLEY'S last work, and worst—until his next;   310
Whether he spin poor couplets into plays,
Or damn the dead with purgatorial praise, [43]
His style in youth or age is still the same,
For ever feeble and for ever tame.
Triumphant first see "Temper's Triumphs" shine!
At least I'm sure they triumphed over mine.
Of "Music's Triumphs," all who read may swear
That luckless Music never triumph'd there. [44]

  Moravians, rise! bestow some meet reward [45]
On dull devotion—Lo! the Sabbath Bard,   320
Sepulchral GRAHAME, [46] pours his notes sublime
In mangled prose, nor e'en aspires to rhyme;
Breaks into blank the Gospel of St. Luke, [xxiii]
And boldly pilfers from the Pentateuch;
And, undisturbed by conscientious qualms,
Perverts the Prophets, and purloins the Psalms.

  Hail, Sympathy! thy soft idea brings" [xxiv]
A thousand visions of a thousand things,
And shows, still whimpering thro' threescore of years, [xxv]
The maudlin prince of mournful sonneteers.   330
And art thou not their prince, harmonious Bowles! [47]
Thou first, great oracle of tender souls?
Whether them sing'st with equal ease, and grief, [xxvi]
The fall of empires, or a yellow leaf;
Whether thy muse most lamentably tells
What merry sounds proceed from Oxford bells, [xxvii]
Or, still in bells delighting, finds a friend
In every chime that jingled from Ostend;
Ah! how much juster were thy Muse's hap,
If to thy bells thou would'st but add a cap! [xxviii]   340
Delightful BOWLES! still blessing and still blest,
All love thy strain, but children like it best.
'Tis thine, with gentle LITTLE'S moral song,

To soothe the mania of the amorous throng!
With thee our nursery damsels shed their tears,
Ere Miss as yet completes her infant years:
But in her teens thy whining powers are vain;
She quits poor BOWLES for LITTLE'S purer strain.
Now to soft themes thou scornest to confine [xxix]
The lofty numbers of a harp like thine; 350
"Awake a louder and a loftier strain," [48]
Such as none heard before, or will again!
Where all discoveries jumbled from the flood,
Since first the leaky ark reposed in mud,
By more or less, are sung in every book,
From Captain Noah down to Captain Cook.
Nor this alone—but, pausing on the road,
The Bard sighs forth a gentle episode, [xxx] [49]
And gravely tells—attend, each beauteous Miss!—
When first Madeira trembled to a kiss. 360
Bowles! in thy memory let this precept dwell,
Stick to thy Sonnets, Man!—at least they sell.
But if some new-born whim, or larger bribe,
Prompt thy crude brain, and claim thee for a scribe:
If 'chance some bard, though once by dunces feared,
Now, prone in dust, can only be revered;
If Pope, whose fame and genius, from the first, [xxxi]
Have foiled the best of critics, needs the worst,
Do thou essay: each fault, each failing scan;
The first of poets was, alas! but man. 370
Rake from each ancient dunghill ev'ry pearl,
Consult Lord Fanny, and confide in CURLL; [50]
Let all the scandals of a former age
Perch on thy pen, and flutter o'er thy page;
Affect a candour which thou canst not feel,
Clothe envy in a garb of honest zeal;
Write, as if St. John's soul could still inspire,
And do from hate what MALLET [51] did for hire.
Oh! hadst thou lived in that congenial time,
To rave with DENNIS, and with RALPH to rhyme; [52] 380
Thronged with the rest around his living head,
Not raised thy hoof against the lion dead,

A meet reward had crowned thy glorious gains,
And linked thee to the Dunciad for thy pains. [53]

   Another Epic! Who inflicts again
More books of blank upon the sons of men?
Boeotian COTTLE, rich Bristowa's boast,
Imports old stories from the Cambrian coast,
And sends his goods to market—all alive!
Lines forty thousand, Cantos twenty-five!   390
Fresh fish from Hippocrene! [54] who'll buy? who'll buy?
The precious bargain's cheap—in faith, not I.
Your turtle-feeder's verse must needs be flat, [xxxii]
Though Bristol bloat him with the verdant fat;
If Commerce fills the purse, she clogs the brain,
And AMOS COTTLE strikes the Lyre in vain.
In him an author's luckless lot behold!
Condemned to make the books which once he sold.
Oh, AMOS COTTLE!—Phoebus! what a name
To fill the speaking-trump of future fame!—   400
Oh, AMOS COTTLE! for a moment think
What meagre profits spring from pen and ink!
When thus devoted to poetic dreams,
Who will peruse thy prostituted reams?
Oh! pen perverted! paper misapplied!
Had COTTLE [55] still adorned the counter's side,
Bent o'er the desk, or, born to useful toils,
Been taught to make the paper which he soils,
Ploughed, delved, or plied the oar with lusty limb,
He had not sung of Wales, nor I of him.   410

   As Sisyphus against the infernal steep
Rolls the huge rock whose motions ne'er may sleep,
So up thy hill, ambrosial Richmond! heaves
Dull MAURICE [56] all his granite weight of leaves:
Smooth, solid monuments of mental pain!
The petrifactions of a plodding brain,
That, ere they reach the top, fall lumbering back again.

   With broken lyre and cheek serenely pale,
Lo! sad Alcæus wanders down the vale;
Though fair they rose, and might have bloomed at last,   420

His hopes have perished by the northern blast:
Nipped in the bud by Caledonian gales,
His blossoms wither as the blast prevails!
O'er his lost works let *classic* SHEFFIELD weep;
May no rude hand disturb their early sleep! [57]

   Yet say! why should the Bard, at once, resign [xxxiii]
His claim to favour from the sacred Nine?
For ever startled by the mingled howl
Of Northern Wolves, that still in darkness prowl;
A coward Brood, which mangle as they prey,   430
By hellish instinct, all that cross their way;
Aged or young, the living or the dead," [xxxiv]
No mercy find-these harpies must be fed.
Why do the injured unresisting yield
The calm possession of their native field?
Why tamely thus before their fangs retreat,
Nor hunt the blood-hounds back to Arthur's Seat? [58]

   Health to immortal JEFFREY! once, in name,
England could boast a judge almost the same; [59]
In soul so like, so merciful, yet just,   440
Some think that Satan has resigned his trust,
And given the Spirit to the world again,
To sentence Letters, as he sentenced men.
With hand less mighty, but with heart as black,
With voice as willing to decree the rack;
Bred in the Courts betimes, though all that law
As yet hath taught him is to find a flaw,—
Since well instructed in the patriot school
To rail at party, though a party tool—
Who knows? if chance his patrons should restore   450
Back to the sway they forfeited before,
His scribbling toils some recompense may meet,
And raise this Daniel to the Judgment-Seat. [60]
Let JEFFREY'S shade indulge the pious hope,
And greeting thus, present him with a rope:
"Heir to my virtues! man of equal mind!
Skilled to condemn as to traduce mankind,
This cord receive! for thee reserved with care,
To wield in judgment, and at length to wear."

  Health to great JEFFREY! Heaven preserve his life,   460
To flourish on the fertile shores of Fife,
And guard it sacred in its future wars,
Since authors sometimes seek the field of Mars!
Can none remember that eventful day, [xxxv] [61]
That ever-glorious, almost fatal fray,
When LITTLE'S leadless pistol met his eye, [62]
And Bow-street Myrmidons stood laughing by?
Oh, day disastrous! on her firm-set rock,
Dunedin's castle felt a secret shock;
Dark rolled the sympathetic waves of Forth,   470
Low groaned the startled whirlwinds of the north;
TWEED ruffled half his waves to form a tear,
The other half pursued his calm career; [63]
ARTHUR'S steep summit nodded to its base,
The surly Tolbooth scarcely kept her place.
The Tolbooth felt—for marble sometimes can,
On such occasions, feel as much as man—
The Tolbooth felt defrauded of his charms,
If JEFFREY died, except within her arms: [64]
Nay last, not least, on that portentous morn,   480
The sixteenth story, where himself was born,
His patrimonial garret, fell to ground,
And pale Edina shuddered at the sound:
Strewed were the streets around with milk-white reams,
Flowed all the Canongate with inky streams;
This of his candour seemed the sable dew,
That of his valour showed the bloodless hue;
And all with justice deemed the two combined
The mingled emblems of his mighty mind.
But Caledonia's goddess hovered o'er   490
The field, and saved him from the wrath of Moore;
From either pistol snatched the vengeful lead,
And straight restored it to her favourite's head;
That head, with greater than magnetic power,
Caught it, as Danäe caught the golden shower,
And, though the thickening dross will scarce refine,
Augments its ore, and is itself a mine.
"My son," she cried, "ne'er thirst for gore again,
Resign the pistol and resume the pen;

O'er politics and poesy preside,   500
Boast of thy country, and Britannia's guide!
For long as Albion's heedless sons submit,
Or Scottish taste decides on English wit,
So long shall last thine unmolested reign,
Nor any dare to take thy name in vain.
Behold, a chosen band shall aid thy plan,
And own thee chieftain of the critic clan.
First in the oat-fed phalanx [65] shall be seen
The travelled Thane, Athenian Aberdeen. [66]
HERBERT shall wield THOR'S hammer, [67] and sometimes   510
In gratitude, thou'lt praise his rugged rhymes.
Smug SYDNEY [68] too thy bitter page shall seek,
And classic HALLAM, [69] much renowned for Greek;
SCOTT may perchance his name and influence lend,
And paltry PILLANS [70] shall traduce his friend;
While gay Thalia's luckless votary, LAMB, [xxxvi] [71]
Damned like the Devil—Devil-like will damn.
Known be thy name! unbounded be thy sway!
Thy HOLLAND'S banquets shall each toil repay!
While grateful Britain yields the praise she owes   520
To HOLLAND'S hirelings and to Learning's foes.
Yet mark one caution ere thy next Review
Spread its light wings of Saffron and of Blue,
Beware lest blundering BROUGHAM [72] destroy the sale,
Turn Beef to Bannocks, Cauliflowers to Kail."
Thus having said, the kilted Goddess kist
Her son, and vanished in a Scottish mist. [73]

   Then prosper, JEFFREY! pertest of the train [74]
Whom Scotland pampers with her fiery grain!
Whatever blessing waits a genuine Scot,   530
In double portion swells thy glorious lot;
For thee Edina culls her evening sweets,
And showers their odours on thy candid sheets,
Whose Hue and Fragrance to thy work adhere—
This scents its pages, and that gilds its rear. [75]
Lo! blushing Itch, coy nymph, enamoured grown,
Forsakes the rest, and cleaves to thee alone,
And, too unjust to other Pictish men,
Enjoys thy person, and inspires thy pen!

Illustrious HOLLAND! hard would be his lot,   540
His hirelings mentioned, and himself forgot! [76]
HOLLAND, with HENRY PETTY [77] at his back,
The whipper-in and huntsman of the pack.
Blest be the banquets spread at Holland House,
Where Scotchmen feed, and Critics may carouse!
Long, long beneath that hospitable roof [xxxvii]
Shall Grub-street dine, while duns are kept aloof.
See honest HALLAM [78] lay aside his fork,
Resume his pen, review his Lordship's work,
And, grateful for the dainties on his plate, [xxxviii]   550
Declare his landlord can at least translate! [79]
Dunedin! view thy children with delight,
They write for food—and feed because they write: [xxxix]
And lest, when heated with the unusual grape,
Some glowing thoughts should to the press escape,
And tinge with red the female reader's cheek,
My lady skims the cream of each critique;
Breathes o'er the page her purity of soul,
Reforms each error, and refines the whole. [80]

   Now to the Drama turn—Oh! motley sight!   560
What precious scenes the wondering eyes invite:
Puns, and a Prince within a barrel pent, [xl] [81]
And Dibdin's nonsense yield complete content. [82]
Though now, thank Heaven! the Rosciomania's o'er. [83]
And full-grown actors are endured once more;
Yet what avail their vain attempts to please,
While British critics suffer scenes like these;
While REYNOLDS vents his "'dammes!'" "poohs!" and
   "zounds!" [xli] [84]
And common-place and common sense confounds?
While KENNEY'S [85] "World"—ah! where is KENNEY'S wit? [xlii]— 570
Tires the sad gallery, lulls the listless Pit;
And BEAUMONT'S pilfered Caratach affords
A tragedy complete in all but words? [xliii]
Who but must mourn, while these are all the rage
The degradation of our vaunted stage?
Heavens! is all sense of shame and talent gone?
Have we no living Bard of merit?—none?
Awake, GEORGE COLMAN! [86] CUMBERLAND, awake![87]

Ring the alarum bell! let folly quake!
Oh! SHERIDAN! if aught can move thy pen,   580
Let Comedy assume her throne again; [xliv]
Abjure the mummery of German schools;
Leave new Pizarros to translating fools; [88]
Give, as thy last memorial to the age,
One classic drama, and reform the stage.
Gods! o'er those boards shall Folly rear her head,
Where GARRICK trod, and SIDDONS lives to tread? [xlv] [89]
On those shall Farce display buffoonery's mask,
And HOOK conceal his heroes in a cask? [90]
Shall sapient managers new scenes produce   590
From CHERRY, [91] SKEFFINGTON, [92] and Mother GOOSE? [xlvi] [93]
While SHAKESPEARE, OTWAY, MASSINGER, forgot,
On stalls must moulder, or in closets rot?
Lo! with what pomp the daily prints proclaim
The rival candidates for Attic fame!
In grim array though LEWIS' spectres rise,
Still SKEFFINGTON and GOOSE divide the prize.
And sure 'great' Skeffington must claim our praise,
For skirtless coats and skeletons of plays
Renowned alike; whose genius ne'er confines   600
Her flight to garnish Greenwood's gay designs; [xlvii] [94]
Nor sleeps with "Sleeping Beauties," but anon
In five facetious acts comes thundering on.
While poor John Bull, bewildered with the scene,
Stares, wondering what the devil it can mean;
But as some hands applaud, a venal few!
Rather than sleep, why John applauds it too.

 Such are we now. Ah! wherefore should we turn
To what our fathers were, unless to mourn?
Degenerate Britons! are ye dead to shame,   610
Or, kind to dulness, do you fear to blame?
Well may the nobles of our present race
Watch each distortion of a NALDI'S face;
Well may they smile on Italy's buffoons,
And worship CATALANI's pantaloons, [95]
Since their own Drama yields no fairer trace
Of wit than puns, of humour than grimace. [96]

    Then let Ausonia, skill'd in every art
To soften manners, but corrupt the heart,
Pour her exotic follies o'er the town,   620
To sanction Vice, and hunt Decorum down:
Let wedded strumpets languish o'er DESHAYES,
And bless the promise which his form displays;
While Gayton bounds before th' enraptured looks
Of hoary Marquises, and stripling Dukes:
Let high-born lechers eye the lively Presle
Twirl her light limbs, that spurn the needless veil;
Let Angiolini bare her breast of snow,
Wave the white arm, and point the pliant toe;
Collini trill her love-inspiring song,   630
Strain her fair neck, and charm the listening throng!
Whet [97] not your scythe, Suppressors of our Vice!
Reforming Saints! too delicately nice!
By whose decrees, our sinful souls to save,
No Sunday tankards foam, no barbers shave;
And beer undrawn, and beards unmown, display
Your holy reverence for the Sabbath-day.

    Or hail at once the patron and the pile
Of vice and folly, Greville and Argyle! [98]
Where yon proud palace, Fashion's hallow'd fane,   640
Spreads wide her portals for the motley train,
Behold the new Petronius [99] of the day, [xlviii]
Our arbiter of pleasure and of play!
There the hired eunuch, the Hesperian choir,
The melting lute, the soft lascivious lyre,
The song from Italy, the step from France,
The midnight orgy, and the mazy dance,
The smile of beauty, and the flush of wine,
For fops, fools, gamesters, knaves, and Lords combine:
Each to his humour—Comus all allows;   650
Champaign, dice, music, or your neighbour's spouse.
Talk not to us, ye starving sons of trade!
Of piteous ruin, which ourselves have made;
In Plenty's sunshine Fortune's minions bask,
Nor think of Poverty, except "en masque," [100]
When for the night some lately titled ass
Appears the beggar which his grandsire was,

The curtain dropped, the gay Burletta o'er,
The audience take their turn upon the floor:
Now round the room the circling dow'gers sweep,   660
Now in loose waltz the thin-clad daughters leap;
The first in lengthened line majestic swim,
The last display the free unfettered limb!
Those for Hibernia's lusty sons repair
With art the charms which Nature could not spare;
These after husbands wing their eager flight,
Nor leave much mystery for the nuptial night.

  Oh! blest retreats of infamy and ease,
Where, all forgotten but the power to please,
Each maid may give a loose to genial thought,   670
Each swain may teach new systems, or be taught:
There the blithe youngster, just returned from Spain,
Cuts the light pack, or calls the rattling main;
The jovial Caster's set, and seven's the Nick,
Or—done!—a thousand on the coming trick!
If, mad with loss, existence 'gins to tire,
And all your hope or wish is to expire,
Here's POWELL'S [101] pistol ready for your life,
And, kinder still, two PAGETS for your wife: [xlix]
Fit consummation of an earthly race   680
Begun in folly, ended in disgrace,
While none but menials o'er the bed of death,
Wash thy red wounds, or watch thy wavering breath;
Traduced by liars, and forgot by all,
The mangled victim of a drunken brawl,
To live like CLODIUS, [102] and like FALKLAND fall.[103]

  Truth! rouse some genuine Bard, and guide his hand
To drive this pestilence from out the land.
E'en I—least thinking of a thoughtless throng,
Just skilled to know the right and choose the wrong,   690
Freed at that age when Reason's shield is lost,
To fight my course through Passion's countless host, [104]
Whom every path of Pleasure's flow'ry way
Has lured in turn, and all have led astray—
E'en I must raise my voice, e'en I must feel
Such scenes, such men, destroy the public weal:

Altho' some kind, censorious friend will say,
"What art thou better, meddling fool, [105] than they?"
And every Brother Rake will smile to see
That miracle, a Moralist in me. 700
No matter—when some Bard in virtue strong,
Gifford perchance, shall raise the chastening song,
Then sleep my pen for ever! and my voice
Be only heard to hail him, and rejoice,
Rejoice, and yield my feeble praise, though I
May feel the lash that Virtue must apply.

    As for the smaller fry, who swarm in shoals
From silly HAFIZ up to simple BOWLES, [106]
Why should we call them from their dark abode,
In Broad St. Giles's or Tottenham-Road? 710
Or (since some men of fashion nobly dare
To scrawl in verse) from Bond-street or the Square? [l]
If things of Ton their harmless lays indite,
Most wisely doomed to shun the public sight,
What harm? in spite of every critic elf,
Sir T. may read his stanzas to himself;
MILES ANDREWS [107] still his strength in couplets try,
And live in prologues, though his dramas die.
Lords too are Bards: such things at times befall,
And 'tis some praise in Peers to write at all. 720
Yet, did or Taste or Reason sway the times,
Ah! who would take their titles with their rhymes? [108]
ROSCOMMON! [109] SHEFFIELD! [110] with your spirits fled, [111]
No future laurels deck a noble head;
No Muse will cheer, with renovating smile,
The paralytic puling of CARLISLE. [li] [112]
The puny schoolboy and his early lay
Men pardon, if his follies pass away;
But who forgives the Senior's ceaseless verse,
Whose hairs grow hoary as his rhymes grow worse? 730
What heterogeneous honours deck the Peer!
Lord, rhymester, petit-maître, pamphleteer! [113]
So dull in youth, so drivelling in his age,
His scenes alone had damned our sinking stage;
But Managers for once cried, "Hold, enough!"
Nor drugged their audience with the tragic stuff.

Yet at their judgment let his Lordship laugh, [lii]
And case his volumes in congenial calf;
Yes! doff that covering, where Morocco shines,
And hang a calf-skin on those recreant lines. [114]   740

   With you, ye Druids! rich in native lead,
Who daily scribble for your daily bread:
With you I war not: GIFFORD'S heavy hand
Has crushed, without remorse, your numerous band.
On "All the Talents" vent your venal spleen; [115]
Want is your plea, let Pity be your screen.
Let Monodies on Fox regale your crew,
And Melville's Mantle [116] prove a Blanket too!
One common Lethe waits each hapless Bard,
And, peace be with you! 'tis your best reward.   750
Such damning fame; as Dunciads only give [liii]
Could bid your lines beyond a morning live;
But now at once your fleeting labours close,
With names of greater note in blest repose.
Far be't from me unkindly to upbraid
The lovely ROSA'S prose in masquerade,
Whose strains, the faithful echoes of her mind,
Leave wondering comprehension far behind. [117]
Though Crusca's bards no more our journals fill, [118]
Some stragglers skirmish round the columns still;   760
Last of the howling host which once was Bell's, [liv]
Matilda snivels yet, and Hafiz yells;
And Merry's [119] metaphors appear anew,
Chained to the signature of O. P. Q. [120]
When some brisk youth, the tenant of a stall,
Employs a pen less pointed than his awl,
Leaves his snug shop, forsakes his store of shoes,
St. Crispin quits, and cobbles for the Muse,
Heavens! how the vulgar stare! how crowds applaud!
How ladies read, and Literati laud! [121]   770
If chance some wicked wag should pass his jest,
'Tis sheer ill-nature—don't the world know best?
Genius must guide when wits admire the rhyme,
And CAPEL LOFFT [122] declares 'tis quite sublime.
Hear, then, ye happy sons of needless trade!
Swains! quit the plough, resign the useless spade!

Lo! BURNS and BLOOMFIELD, nay, a greater far,
GIFFORD was born beneath an adverse star,
Forsook the labours of a servile state,
Stemmed the rude storm, and triumphed over Fate: 780
Then why no more? if Phoebus smiled on you,
BLOOMFIELD! why not on brother Nathan too? [123]
Him too the Mania, not the Muse, has seized;
Not inspiration, but a mind diseased:
And now no Boor can seek his last abode,
No common be inclosed without an ode.
Oh! since increased refinement deigns to smile
On Britain's sons, and bless our genial Isle,
Let Poesy go forth, pervade the whole,
Alike the rustic, and mechanic soul!   790
Ye tuneful cobblers! still your notes prolong,
Compose at once a slipper and a song;
So shall the fair your handywork peruse,
Your sonnets sure shall please—perhaps your shoes.
May Moorland weavers [124] boast Pindaric skill,
And tailors' lays be longer than their bill!
While punctual beaux reward the grateful notes,
And pay for poems—when they pay for coats.

    To the famed throng now paid the tribute due, [lv]
Neglected Genius! let me turn to you.   800
Come forth, oh CAMPBELL! give thy talents scope;
Who dares aspire if thou must cease to hope?
And thou, melodious ROGERS! rise at last,
Recall the pleasing memory of the past; [125]
Arise! let blest remembrance still inspire,
And strike to wonted tones thy hallowed lyre;
Restore Apollo to his vacant throne,
Assert thy country's honour and thine own.
What! must deserted Poesy still weep
Where her last hopes with pious COWPER sleep?   810
Unless, perchance, from his cold bier she turns,
To deck the turf that wraps her minstrel, BURNS!
No! though contempt hath marked the spurious brood,
The race who rhyme from folly, or for food,
Yet still some genuine sons 'tis hers to boast,
Who, least affecting, still affect the most: [lvi]

Feel as they write, and write but as they feel—
Bear witness GIFFORD, [126] SOTHEBY, [127] MACNEIL. [128]
"Why slumbers GIFFORD?" once was asked in vain;
Why slumbers GIFFORD? let us ask again. [129]   820
Are there no follies for his pen to purge?
Are there no fools whose backs demand the scourge?
Are there no sins for Satire's Bard to greet?
Stalks not gigantic Vice in every street?
Shall Peers or Princes tread pollution's path,
And 'scape alike the Laws and Muse's wrath?
Nor blaze with guilty glare through future time,
Eternal beacons of consummate crime?
Arouse thee, GIFFORD! be thy promise claimed,
Make bad men better, or at least ashamed.   830

   Unhappy WHITE! [130] while life was in its spring,
And thy young Muse just waved her joyous wing,
The Spoiler swept that soaring Lyre away, [lvii] [131]
Which else had sounded an immortal lay.
Oh! what a noble heart was here undone,
When Science' self destroyed her favourite son!
Yes, she too much indulged thy fond pursuit,
She sowed the seeds, but Death has reaped the fruit.
'Twas thine own Genius gave the final blow,
And helped to plant the wound that laid thee low: 840
So the struck Eagle, stretched upon the plain,
No more through rolling clouds to soar again,
Viewed his own feather on the fatal dart,
And winged the shaft that quivered in his heart;
Keen were his pangs, but keener far to feel
He nursed the pinion which impelled the steel;
While the same plumage that had warmed his nest
Drank the last life-drop of his bleeding breast.

   There be who say, in these enlightened days,
That splendid lies are all the poet's praise;   850
That strained Invention, ever on the wing,
Alone impels the modern Bard to sing:
Tis true, that all who rhyme—nay, all who write,
Shrink from that fatal word to Genius—Trite;
Yet Truth sometimes will lend her noblest fires,

And decorate the verse herself inspires:
This fact in Virtue's name let CRABBE [132] attest;
Though Nature's sternest Painter, yet the best.

   And here let SHEE [133] and Genius find a place,
Whose pen and pencil yield an equal grace;   860
To guide whose hand the sister Arts combine,
And trace the Poet's or the Painter's line;
Whose magic touch can bid the canvas glow,
Or pour the easy rhyme's harmonious flow;
While honours, doubly merited, attend [lviii]
The Poet's rival, but the Painter's friend.

   Blest is the man who dares approach the bower
Where dwelt the Muses at their natal hour;
Whose steps have pressed, whose eye has marked afar,
The clime that nursed the sons of song and war,   870
The scenes which Glory still must hover o'er,
Her place of birth, her own Achaian shore.
But doubly blest is he whose heart expands
With hallowed feelings for those classic lands;
Who rends the veil of ages long gone by,
And views their remnants with a poet's eye!
WRIGHT! [134] 'twas thy happy lot at once to view
Those shores of glory, and to sing them too;
And sure no common Muse inspired thy pen
To hail the land of Gods and Godlike men.   880

   And you, associate Bards! [135] who snatched to light [lvix]
Those gems too long withheld from modern sight;
Whose mingling taste combined to cull the wreath
While Attic flowers Aonian odours breathe,
And all their renovated fragrance flung,
To grace the beauties of your native tongue;
Now let those minds, that nobly could transfuse
The glorious Spirit of the Grecian Muse,
Though soft the echo, scorn a borrowed tone: [lx]
Resign Achaia's lyre, and strike your own.   890

   Let these, or such as these, with just applause, [lxi]
Restore the Muse's violated laws;

But not in flimsy DARWIN'S [136] pompous chime, [lxii]
That mighty master of unmeaning rhyme,
Whose gilded cymbals, more adorned than clear,
The eye delighted, but fatigued the ear,
In show the simple lyre could once surpass,
But now, worn down, appear in native brass;
While all his train of hovering sylphs around
Evaporate in similes and sound: 900
Him let them shun, with him let tinsel die:
False glare attracts, but more offends the eye. [137]

    Yet let them not to vulgar WORDSWORTH [138] stoop,
The meanest object of the lowly group,
Whose verse, of all but childish prattle void,
Seems blessed harmony to LAMB and LLOYD: [139]
Let them—but hold, my Muse, nor dare to teach
A strain far, far beyond thy humble reach:
The native genius with their being given
Will point the path, and peal their notes to heaven.   910

    And thou, too, SCOTT! [140] resign to minstrels rude
The wilder Slogan of a Border feud:
Let others spin their meagre lines for hire;
Enough for Genius, if itself inspire!
Let SOUTHEY sing, altho' his teeming muse, [lxiii]
Prolific every spring, be too profuse;
Let simple WORDSWORTH [141] chime his childish verse,
And brother COLERIDGE lull the babe at nurse [lxiv]
Let Spectre-mongering LEWIS aim, at most, [lxv]
To rouse the Galleries, or to raise a ghost;   920
Let MOORE still sigh; let STRANGFORD steal from MOORE, [lxvi]
And swear that CAMOËNS sang such notes of yore;
Let HAYLEY hobble on, MONTGOMERY rave,
And godly GRAHAME chant a stupid stave;
Let sonneteering BOWLES [142] his strains refine,
And whine and whimper to the fourteenth line;
Let STOTT, CARLISLE, [143] MATILDA, and the rest
Of Grub Street, and of Grosvenor Place the best,
Scrawl on, 'till death release us from the strain,
Or Common Sense assert her rights again;   930
But Thou, with powers that mock the aid of praise,

Should'st leave to humbler Bards ignoble lays:
Thy country's voice, the voice of all the Nine,
Demand a hallowed harp—that harp is thine.
Say! will not Caledonia's annals yield
The glorious record of some nobler field,
Than the vile foray of a plundering clan,
Whose proudest deeds disgrace the name of man?
Or Marmion's acts of darkness, fitter food
For SHERWOOD'S outlaw tales of ROBIN HOOD? [lxvii]   940
Scotland! still proudly claim thy native Bard,
And be thy praise his first, his best reward!
Yet not with thee alone his name should live,
But own the vast renown a world can give;
Be known, perchance, when Albion is no more,
And tell the tale of what she was before;
To future times her faded fame recall,
And save her glory, though his country fall.

   Yet what avails the sanguine Poet's hope,
To conquer ages, and with time to cope?   950
New eras spread their wings, new nations rise,
And other Victors fill th' applauding skies; [144]
A few brief generations fleet along,
Whose sons forget the Poet and his song:
E'en now, what once-loved Minstrels scarce may claim
The transient mention of a dubious name!
When Fame's loud trump hath blown its noblest blast,
Though long the sound, the echo sleeps at last;
And glory, like the Phoenix [145] midst her fires,
Exhales her odours, blazes, and expires.   960

   Shall hoary Granta call her sable sons,
Expert in science, more expert at puns?
Shall these approach the Muse? ah, no! she flies,
Even from the tempting ore of Seaton's prize; [lxviii]
Though Printers condescend the press to soil
With rhyme by HOARE, [146] and epic blank by HOYLE: [lxix] [147]
Not him whose page, if still upheld by whist,
Requires no sacred theme to bid us list. [148]
Ye! who in Granta's honours would surpass,
Must mount her Pegasus, a full-grown ass;   970

A foal well worthy of her ancient Dam,
Whose Helicon [149] is duller than her Cam. [lxx]

   There CLARKE, [150] still striving piteously "to please," [lxxi]
Forgetting doggerel leads not to degrees,
A would-be satirist, a hired Buffoon,
A monthly scribbler of some low Lampoon, [151]
Condemned to drudge, the meanest of the mean,
And furbish falsehoods for a magazine,
Devotes to scandal his congenial mind;
Himself a living libel on mankind.   980

   Oh! dark asylum of a Vandal race! [152]
At once the boast of learning, and disgrace!
So lost to Phoebus, that nor Hodgson's [153] verse
Can make thee better, nor poor Hewson's [154] worse. [lxxii]
But where fair Isis rolls her purer wave,
The partial Muse delighted loves to lave;
On her green banks a greener wreath she wove, [lxxiii]
To crown the Bards that haunt her classic grove;
Where RICHARDS wakes a genuine poet's fires,
And modern Britons glory in their Sires. [155] [lxxiv]   990

   For me, who, thus unasked, have dared to tell
My country, what her sons should know too well, [lxxv]
Zeal for her honour bade me here engage [lxxvi]
The host of idiots that infest her age;
No just applause her honoured name shall lose,
As first in freedom, dearest to the Muse.
Oh! would thy bards but emulate thy fame,
And rise more worthy, Albion, of thy name!
What Athens was in science, Rome in power,
What Tyre appeared in her meridian hour,   1000
'Tis thine at once, fair Albion! to have been—
Earth's chief Dictatress, Ocean's lovely Queen: [lxxvii]
But Rome decayed, and Athens strewed the plain,
And Tyre's proud piers lie shattered in the main;
Like these, thy strength may sink, in ruin hurled, [lxxviii]
And Britain fall, the bulwark of the world.
But let me cease, and dread Cassandra's fate,
With warning ever scoffed at, till too late;

To themes less lofty still my lay confine,
And urge thy Bards to gain a name like thine. [156]   1010

   Then, hapless Britain! be thy rulers blest,
The senate's oracles, the people's jest!
Still hear thy motley orators dispense
The flowers of rhetoric, though not of sense,
While CANNING'S colleagues hate him for his wit,
And old dame PORTLAND [157] fills the place of PITT.

   Yet once again, adieu! ere this the sail
That wafts me hence is shivering in the gale;
And Afric's coast and Calpe's adverse height, [158]
And Stamboul's minarets must greet my sight: 1020
Thence shall I stray through Beauty's native clime, [159]
Where Kaff [160] is clad in rocks, and crowned with snows sublime.
But should I back return, no tempting press [lxxix]
Shall drag my Journal from the desk's recess;
Let coxcombs, printing as they come from far,
Snatch his own wreath of Ridicule from Carr;
Let ABERDEEN and ELGIN [161] still pursue
The shade of fame through regions of Virtù;
Waste useless thousands on their Phidian freaks,
Misshapen monuments and maimed antiques;   1030
And make their grand saloons a general mart
For all the mutilated blocks of art:
Of Dardan tours let Dilettanti tell,
I leave topography to rapid [162] GELL; [163]
And, quite content, no more shall interpose
To stun the public ear—at least with Prose. [lxxx]

   Thus far I've held my undisturbed career,
Prepared for rancour, steeled 'gainst selfish fear;
This thing of rhyme I ne'er disdained to own—
Though not obtrusive, yet not quite unknown: 1040
My voice was heard again, though not so loud,
My page, though nameless, never disavowed;
And now at once I tear the veil away:—
Cheer on the pack! the Quarry stands at bay,
Unscared by all the din of MELBOURNE house, [164]
By LAMB'S resentment, or by HOLLAND'S spouse,

By JEFFREY'S harmless pistol, HALLAM'S rage,
Edina's brawny sons and brimstone page.
Our men in buckram shall have blows enough,
And feel they too are "penetrable stuff:" 1050
And though I hope not hence unscathed to go,
Who conquers me shall find a stubborn foe.
The time hath been, when no harsh sound would fall
From lips that now may seem imbued with gall;
Nor fools nor follies tempt me to despise
The meanest thing that crawled beneath my eyes:
But now, so callous grown, so changed since youth,
I've learned to think, and sternly speak the truth;
Learned to deride the critic's starch decree,
And break him on the wheel he meant for me; 1060
To spurn the rod a scribbler bids me kiss,
Nor care if courts and crowds applaud or hiss:
Nay more, though all my rival rhymesters frown,
I too can hunt a Poetaster down;
And, armed in proof, the gauntlet cast at once
To Scotch marauder, and to Southern dunce.
Thus much I've dared; if my incondite lay [lxxx]
Hath wronged these righteous times, let others say:
This, let the world, which knows not how to spare,
Yet rarely blames unjustly, now declare. [165] 1070

Footnotes:

[Footnote 1: "The 'binding' of this volume is considerably too valuable for the contents. Nothing but the consideration of its being the property of another, prevents me from consigning this miserable record of misplaced anger and indiscriminate acrimony to the flames."—B., 1816.]

[Footnote 2: IMITATION.

"Semper ego auditor tantum? nunquamne reponam,
Vexatus toties, rauci Theseide Codri?"

JUVENAL, 'Satire I'.l. 1.]

[Footnote 3: "'Hoarse Fitzgerald'.—"Right enough; but why notice such a mountebank?"—B., 1816.

Mr. Fitzgerald, facetiously termed by Cobbett the "Small Beer Poet," inflicts his annual tribute of verse on the Literary Fund: not content with writing, he spouts in person, after the company have imbibed a reasonable quantity of bad port, to enable them to sustain the operation.

[William Thomas Fitzgerald (circ. 1759-1829) played the part of unofficial poet laureate. His loyal recitations were reported by the newspapers. He published, 'inter alia', 'Nelson's Triumph' (1798), 'Tears of Hibernia, dispelled by the Union' (1802), and 'Nelson's Tomb' (1806). He owes his fame to the first line of 'English Bards', and the famous parody in 'Rejected Addresses'. The following 'jeux désprits' were transcribed by R. C. Dallas on a blank leaf of a copy of the Fifth Edition:—

"Written on a copy of 'English Bards' at the 'Alfred' by W. T. Fitzgerald, Esq.—

I find Lord Byron scorns my Muse,
Our Fates are ill agreed;
The Verse is safe, I can't abuse
Those lines, I never read.

Signed W. T. F."

Answer written on the same page by Lord Byron—

"What's writ on me," cries Fitz, "I never read"!
What's writ by thee, dear Fitz, none will, indeed.
The case stands simply thus, then, honest Fitz,
Thou and thine enemies are fairly quits;
Or rather would be, if for time to come,
They luckily were 'deaf', or thou wert dumb;
But to their pens while scribblers add their tongues.
The Waiter only can escape their lungs. [A]]

{Sub-Footnote 0.1: Compare 'Hints from Horace', l. 808, 'note' 1.}

[Footnote 4: Cid Hamet Benengeli promises repose to his pen, in the last chapter of 'Don Quixote'. Oh! that our voluminous gentry would follow the example of Cid Hamet Benengeli!]

[Footnote 5: "This must have been written in the spirit of prophecy." (B., 1816.)]

[Footnote 6: "He's a very good fellow; and, except his mother and sister, the best of the set, to my mind."—B., 1816. [William (1779-1848) and George (1784-1834) Lamb, sons of Sir Peniston Lamb (Viscount Melbourne, 1828), by Elizabeth, only daughter of Sir Ralph Milbanke, were Lady Byron's first cousins. William married, in 1805, Lady Caroline Ponsonby, the writer of 'Glenarvon'. George, who was one of the early contributors to the 'Edinburgh Review', married in 1809 Caroline Rosalie Adelaide St. Jules. At the time of the separation, Lady Caroline Lamb and Mrs. George Lamb warmly espoused Lady Byron's cause, Lady Melbourne and her daughter Lady Cowper (afterwards Lady Palmerston) were rather against than for Lady Byron. William Lamb was discreetly silent, and George Lamb declaimed against Lady Byron, calling her a d———d fool. Hence Lord Byron's praises of George. Cf. line 517 of 'English Bards'.]

[Footnote 7: This ingenuous youth is mentioned more particularly, with his production, in another place. ('Vide post', l. 516.)

"Spurious Brat" [see variant ii. p. 300], that is the farce; the ingenuous youth who begat it is mentioned more particularly with his offspring in another place. ['Note. MS. M.'] [The farce 'Whistle for It' was performed two or three times at Covent Garden Theatre in 1807.]

[Footnote 8: In the 'Edinburgh Review'.]

[Footnote 9: The proverbial "Joe" Miller, an actor by profession (1684-1738), was a man of no education, and is said to have been unable to read. His reputation rests mainly on the book of jests compiled after his death, and attributed to him by John Mottley. (First Edition. T. Read. 1739.)]

[Footnote 10: Messrs. Jeffrey and Lamb are the alpha and omega, the first and last of the 'Edinburgh Review'; the others are mentioned hereafter.

[The MS. Note is as follows:—"Of the young gentlemen who write in the 'E.R.', I have now named the alpha and omega, the first and the last, the best and the worst. The intermediate members are designated with due honour hereafter."]

"This was not just. Neither the heart nor the head of these gentlemen are at all what they are here represented. At the time this was written, I was personally unacquainted with either."—B., 1816.

[Francis Jeffrey (1773-1850) founded the 'Edinburgh Review' in conjunction with Sydney Smith, Brougham, and Francis Horner, in 1802. In 1803 he succeeded Smith as editor, and conducted the 'Review' till 1829. Independence of publishers and high pay to contributors ("Ten guineas a sheet," writes Southey to Scott, June, 1807, "instead of seven pounds for the 'Annual'," 'Life and Corr'., iii. 125) distinguished the new journal from the first. Jeffrey was called to the Scottish bar in 1794, and as an advocate was especially successful with juries. He was constantly employed, and won fame and fortune. In 1829 he was elected Dean of the Faculty of Advocates, and the following year, when the Whigs came into office, he became Lord Advocate. He sat as M.P. twice for Malton (1830-1832), and, afterwards, for Edinburgh. In 1834 he was appointed a Judge of the Court of Sessions, when he took the title of Lord Jeffrey. Byron had attacked Jeffrey in British Bards before his 'Hours of Idleness' had been cut up by the 'Edinburgh', and when the article appeared (Jan. 1808), under the mistaken impression that he was the author, denounced him at large (ll. 460-528) in the first edition of 'English Bards, and Scotch Reviewers'. None the less, the great critic did not fail to do ample justice to the poet's mature work, and won from him repeated acknowledgments of his kindness and generosity. (See 'Edinburgh Review', vol. xxii. p. 416, and Byron's comment in his 'Diary' for March 20,1814; 'Life', p. 232. See, too, 'Hints from Horace', ll. 589-626; and 'Don Juan', canto x. st. 11-16, and canto xii. st. 16. See also Bagehot's 'Literary Studies', vol. i. article I.)]

[Footnote 11: IMITATION.

"Stulta est dementia, cum tot ubique ————occurras periturae parcere chartae."

JUVENAL, 'Sat. I.' ll. 17, 18.]

[Footnote 12: IMITATION.

"Cur tamen hoc potius libeat decurrere campo,
Per quem magnus equos Auruncæ flexit alumnus,
Si vacat, et placidi rationem admittitis, edam."

JUVENAL, 'Sat. I'. ll. 19-21.]

[Footnote 13: William Gifford (1756-1826), a self-taught scholar, first a ploughboy, then boy on board a Brixham coaster, afterwards shoemaker's apprentice, was sent by friends to Exeter College, Oxford (1779-81). In the 'Baviad' (1794) and the 'Maeviad' (1795) he attacked many of the smaller writers of the day, who were either silly, like the Della Cruscan School, or discreditable, like Williams, who wrote as "Anthony Pasquin." In his 'Epistle to Peter Pindar' (1800) he laboured to expose the true character of John Wolcot. As editor of the 'Anti-Jacobin, or Weekly Examiner' (November, 1797, to July, 1798), he supported the political views of Canning and his friends. As editor of the 'Quarterly Review', from its foundation (February, 1809) to his resignation in September, 1824, he soon rose to literary eminence by his sound sense and adherence to the best models, though his judgments were sometimes narrow-minded and warped by political prejudice. His editions of 'Massinger' (1805), which superseded that of Monck Mason and Davies (1765), of 'Ben Jonson' (1816), of 'Ford' (1827), are valuable. To his translation of 'Juvenal' (1802) is prefixed his autobiography. His translation of 'Persius' appeared in 1821. To Gifford, Byron usually paid the utmost deference. "Any suggestion of yours, even if it were conveyed," he writes to him, in 1813, "in the less tender text of the 'Baviad', or a Monck Mason note to Massinger, would be obeyed." See also his letter (September 20, 1821, 'Life', p.531): "I know no praise which would compensate me in my own mind for his censure." Byron was attracted to Gifford, partly by his devotion to the classical models of literature, partly by the outspoken frankness of his literary criticism, partly also, perhaps, by his physical deformity.]

[Footnote 14: Henry James Pye (1745-1813), M.P. for Berkshire, and afterwards Police Magistrate for Westminster, held the office of poet laureate from 1790 till his death in 1813, succeeding Thomas Warton, and succeeded by Southey. He published 'Farringdon Hill' in 1774, The 'Progress of Refinement' in 1783, and a translation of Burger's 'Lenore' in 1795. His name recurs in the 'Vision of Judgment', stanza xcii. Lines 97-102 were inserted in the Fifth Edition.]

[Footnote 15: The first edition of the Satire opened with this line; and Byron's original intention was to prefix the following argument, first published in 'Recollections', by R. C. Dallas (1824):—

"ARGUMENT.

"The poet considereth times past, and their poesy—makes a sudden transition to times present—is incensed against book-makers—revileth Walter Scott for cupidity and ballad-mongering, with notable remarks on Master Southey—complaineth that Master Southey had inflicted three poems, epic and otherwise, on the public—inveigheth against William Wordsworth, but laudeth Mister Coleridge and his elegy on a young ass—is disposed to vituperate Mr. Lewis—and greatly rebuketh Thomas Little (the late) and Lord Strangford—recommendeth Mr. Hayley to turn his attention to prose—and exhorteth the Moravians to glorify Mr. Grahame—sympathiseth with the Rev. [William Bowles]—and deploreth the melancholy fate of James Montgomery—breaketh out into invective against the Edinburgh Reviewers—calleth them hard names, harpies and the like—apostrophiseth Jeffrey, and prophesieth.—Episode of Jeffrey and Moore, their jeopardy and deliverance; portents on the morn of the combat; the Tweed, Tolbooth, Firth of Forth [and Arthur's Seat], severally shocked; descent of a goddess to save Jeffrey; incorporation of the bullets with his sinciput and occiput.—Edinburgh Reviews 'en masse'.—Lord Aberdeen, Herbert, Scott, Hallam, Pillans, Lambe, Sydney Smith, Brougham, etc.—Lord Holland applauded for dinners and translations.—The Drama; Skeffington, Hook, Reynolds, Kenney, Cherry, etc.—Sheridan, Colman, and Cumberland called upon [requested, MS.] to write.—Return to poesy—scribblers of all sorts—lords sometimes rhyme; much better not—Hafiz, Rosa Matilda, and X.Y.Z.—Rogers, Campbell, Gifford, etc. true poets—Translators of the Greek Anthology—Crabbe—Darwin's style—Cambridge—Seatonian Prize—Smythe—Hodgson—Oxford—Richards—Poetaloquitur—Conclusion."]

[Footnote 16: Lines 115, 116, were a MS. addition to the printed text of 'British Bards'. An alternative version has been pencilled on the margin:—

"Otway and Congreve mimic scenes had wove
And Waller tuned his Lyre to mighty Love."]

[Footnote 17: Thomas Little was the name under which Moore's early poems were published, 'The Poetical Works of the late Thomas Little, Esq.' (1801). "Twelves" refers to the "duodecimo." Sheets, after printing, are pressed between cold or hot rollers, to impart smoothness of "surface." Hot rolling is the more expensive process.]

[Footnote 18: Eccles. chapter i. verse 9.]

[Footnote 19: At first sight Byron appears to refer to the lighting of streets by gas, especially as the first shop lighted with it was that of Lardner & Co., at the corner of the Albany (June, 1805), and as lamps were on view at the premises of the Gas Light and Coke Company in Pall Mall from 1808 onwards. But it is almost certain that he alludes to the "sublimating gas" of Dr. Beddoes, which his assistant, Davy, mentions in his 'Researches' (1800) as nitrous oxide, and which was used by Southey and Coleridge. The same four "wonders" of medical science are depicted in Gillray's caricatures, November, 1801, and May and June, 1802, and are satirized in Christopher Caustic's 'Terrible Tractoration! A Poetical Petition against Galvanising Trumpery and the Perkinistit Institution' (in 4 cantos, 1803).

Against vaccination, or cow-pox, a brisk war was still being carried on. Gillray has a likeness of Jenner vaccinating patients.

Metallic "Tractors" were a remedy much advertised at the beginning of the century by an American quack, Benjamin Charles Perkins, founder of the Perkinean Institution in London, as a "cure for all Disorders, Red Noses, Gouty Toes, Windy Bowels, Broken Legs, Hump Backs."

In Galvanism several experiments, conducted by Professor Aldini, nephew of Galvani, are described in the 'Morning Post' for Jan. 6th, Feb. 6th, and Jan. 22nd, 1803. The latter were made on the body of Forster the murderer.

For the allusion to Gas, compare 'Terrible Tractoration', canto 1—

"Beddoes (bless the good doctor) has
Sent me a bag full of his gas,
Which snuff'd the nose up, makes wit brighter,
And eke a dunce an airy writer."]

[Footnote 20: Stott, better known in the 'Morning Post' by the name of Hafiz. This personage is at present the most profound explorer of the bathos. I remember, when the reigning family left Portugal, a special Ode of Master Stott's, beginning thus:—('Stott loquitur quoad Hibernia')—

"Princely offspring of Braganza,
Erin greets thee with a stanza," etc.

Also a Sonnet to Rats, well worthy of the subject, and a most thundering Ode, commencing as follows:—

"Oh! for a Lay! loud as the surge
That lashes Lapland's sounding shore."

Lord have mercy on us! the "Lay of the Last Minstrel" was nothing to this. [The lines "Princely Offspring," headed "Extemporaneous Verse on the expulsion of the Prince Regent from Portugal by Gallic Tyranny," were published in the 'Morning Post', Dec. 30, 1807. (See 'post', l. 708, and 'note'.)]]

[Footnote 21: See p. 317, note 1.]

[Footnote 22: See the "Lay of the Last Minstrel," 'passim'. Never was any plan so incongruous and absurd as the groundwork of this production. The entrance of Thunder and Lightning prologuising to Bayes' tragedy [('vide The Rehearsal'), 'British Bards'], unfortunately takes away the merit of originality from the dialogue between Messieurs the Spirits of Flood and Fell in the first canto. Then we have the amiable William of Deloraine, "a stark moss-trooper," videlicet, a happy compound of poacher, sheep-stealer, and highwayman. The propriety of his magical lady's injunction not to read can only be equalled by his candid acknowledgment of his independence of the trammels of spelling, although, to use his own elegant phrase, "'twas his neckverse at Harribee," 'i. e.' the gallows.

The biography of Gilpin Horner, and the marvellous pedestrian page, who travelled twice as fast as his master's horse, without the aid of seven-leagued boots, are 'chefs d'oeuvre' in the improvement of taste. For incident we have the invisible, but by no means sparing box on the ear bestowed on the page, and the entrance of a Knight and Charger into the castle, under the very natural disguise of a wain of hay. Marmion, the hero of the latter romance, is exactly what William of Deloraine would have been, had he been able to read and write. The poem was manufactured for Messrs. CONSTABLE, MURRAY, and MILLER, worshipful Booksellers, in consideration of the receipt of a sum of money; and truly, considering the inspiration, it is a very creditable production. If Mr. SCOTT will write for hire, let him do his best for his paymasters, but not disgrace his genius, which is undoubtedly great, by a repetition of Black-Letter Ballad imitations.

[Constable paid Scott a thousand pounds for 'Marmion', and

"offered one fourth of the copyright to Mr. Miller of Albemarle Street, and one fourth to Mr. Murray of Fleet Street (see line 173). Both publishers eagerly accepted the proposal."
...
"A severe and unjust review of 'Marmion' by Jeffrey appeared in [the 'Edinburgh Review' for April] 1808, accusing Scott of a mercenary spirit in writing for money. ... Scott was much nettled by these observations."

('Memoirs of John Murray', i. 76, 95). In his diary of 1813 Byron wrote of Scott,

"He is undoubtedly the Monarch of Parnassus, and the most 'English' of Bards."

'Life', p. 206.]]

[Footnote 23: It was the suggestion of the Countess of Dalkeith, that Scott should write a ballad on the old border legend of 'Gilpin Horner', which first gave shape to the poet's ideas, and led to the 'Lay of the Last Minstrel'.]

[Footnote 24: In his strictures on Scott and Southey, Byron takes his lead from Lady Anne Hamilton's (1766-1846, daughter of Archibald, ninth Duke of Hamilton, and Lady-in-waiting to Caroline of Brunswick) 'Epics of the Ton' (1807), a work which has not shared the dubious celebrity of her 'Secret Memories of the Court', etc. (1832). Compare the following lines (p. 9):—

"Then still might Southey sing his crazy Joan,
Or feign a Welshman o'er the Atlantic flown,
Or tell of Thalaba the wondrous matter,
Or with clown Wordsworth, chatter, chatter, chatter.
       * * * * *
Good-natured Scott rehearse, in well-paid lays,
The marv'lous chiefs and elves of other days."

(For Scott's reference to "my share of flagellation among my betters," and an explicit statement that he had remonstrated with Jeffrey against the "offensive criticism" of 'Hours of Idleness', because he thought it treated with undue severity, see Introduction to 'Marmion', 1830.)]]

[Footnote 25: Lines 179, 180, in the Fifth Edition, were substituted for variant i. p. 312.— 'Leigh Hunt's annotated Copy of the Fourth Edition'.]

[Footnote 26: "Good night to Marmion"—the pathetic and also prophetic exclamation of Henry Blount, Esquire, on the death of honest Marmion.]

[Footnote 27: As the 'Odyssey' is so closely connected with the story of the 'Iliad', they may almost be classed as one grand historical poem. In alluding to Milton and Tasso, we consider the 'Paradise Lost' and 'Gerusalemme Liberata' as their standard efforts; since neither the 'Jerusalem Conquered' of the Italian, nor the 'Paradise Regained' of the English bard, obtained a proportionate celebrity to their former poems. Query: Which of Mr. Southey's will survive?]

[Footnote 28: 'Thalaba', Mr. Southey's second poem, is written in defiance of precedent and poetry. Mr. S. wished to produce something novel, and succeeded to a miracle. 'Joan of Arc' was marvellous enough, but 'Thalaba' was one of those poems "which," in the word of PORSON, "will be read when Homer and Virgil are forgotten, but—<i<not till then'." ["Of 'Thalaba" the wild and wondrous song"—Proem to 'Madoc', Southey's 'Poetical Works' (1838), vol. v. 'Joan of Arc' was published in 1796, 'Thalaba the Destroyer' in 1801, and 'Madoc' in 1805.]

[Footnote 29: The hero of Fielding's farce, 'The Tragedy of Tragedies', 'or the Life and Death of Tom Thumb the Great', first played in 1730 at the Haymarket.]

[Footnote 30: Southey's 'Madoc' is divided into two parts—Part I., "Madoc in Wales;" Part II., "Madoc in Aztlan." The word "cacique" ("Cacique or cazique... a native chief or 'prince' of the aborigines in the West Indies:" 'New Engl. Dict'., Art. "Cacique") occurs in the translations of Spanish writers quoted by Southey in his notes, but not in the text of the poem.]

[Footnote 31: We beg Mr. Southey's pardon: "Madoc disdains the degraded title of Epic." See his Preface. ["It assumes not the degraded title of Epic."—Preface to 'Madoc' (1805), Southey's 'Poetical Works' (1838), vol. v. p. xxi.] Why is Epic degraded? and by whom? Certainly the late Romaunts of Masters Cottle, Laureat Pye, Ogilvy, Hole,[A] and gentle Mistress Cowley, have not exalted the Epic Muse; but, as Mr. SOUTHEY'S poem "disdains the appellation," allow us to ask—has he substituted anything better in its stead? or must he be content to rival Sir RICHARD BLACKMORE in the quantity as well as quality of his verse?

[Sub-Footnote A: For "Hole," the 'MS'. and 'British Bards' read "Sir J. B. Burgess; Cumberland."]]

[Footnote 32: See 'The Old Woman of Berkeley', a ballad by Mr. Southey, wherein an aged gentlewoman is carried away by Beelzebub, on a "high trotting horse."]

[Footnote 33: The last line, "God help thee," is an evident plagiarism from the 'Anti-Jacobin' to Mr. Southey, on his Dactylics:—

"God help thee, silly one!"

'Poetry of the Anti-Jacobin', p. 23.]

[Footnote 34: In the annotated copy of the Fourth Edition Byron has drawn a line down the margin of the passage on Wordsworth, lines 236-248, and adds the word "Unjust." The first four lines on Coleridge (lines 255-258) are also marked "Unjust." The recantation is, no doubt, intended to apply to both passages from beginning to end. "'Unjust'."—B., 1816. (See also Byron's letter to S. T. Coleridge, March 31, 1815.)]

[Footnote 35: 'Lyrical Ballads', p. 4.—"The Tables Turned," Stanza 1.

"Up, up, my friend, and clear your looks,
Why all this toil and trouble?
Up, up, my friend, and quit your books,
Or surely you'll grow double."]

[Footnote 36: Mr. W. in his preface labours hard to prove, that prose and verse are much the same; and certainly his precepts and practice are strictly conformable:—

"And thus to Betty's questions he
Made answer, like a traveller bold.
'The cock did crow, to-whoo, to-whoo,
And the sun did shine so cold.'"

'Lyrical Ballads', p. 179. [Compare 'The Simpliciad', ll. 295-305, and 'note'.]]

[Footnote 37: "He has not published for some years."—'British Bards'. (A marginal note in pencil.) [Coleridge's 'Poems' (3rd edit.) appeared in 1803; the first number of 'The Friend' on June 1, 1809.]]

[Footnote 38: COLERIDGE'S 'Poems', p. 11, "Songs of the Pixies," 'i. e.' Devonshire Fairies; p. 42, we have "Lines to a Young Lady;" and, p. 52, "Lines to a Young Ass." [Compare 'The Simpliciad', ll. 211, 213—

"Then in despite of scornful Folly's pother,
Ask him to live with you and hail him brother."]]

[Footnote 39: Matthew Gregory Lewis (1775-1818), known as "Monk" Lewis, was the son of a rich Jamaica planter. During a six months' visit to Weimar (1792-3), when he was introduced to Goethe, he applied himself to the study of German literature, especially novels and the drama. In 1794 he was appointed 'attaché' to the Embassy at the Hague, and in the course of ten weeks wrote 'Ambrosio, or The Monk', which was published in 1795. In 1798 he made the acquaintance of Scott, and procured his promise of co-operation in his contemplated 'Tales of Terror'. In the same year he published the 'Castle Spectre' (first played at Drury Lane, Dec. 14, 1797), in which, to quote the postscript "To the Reader," he meant (but Sheridan interposed) "to have exhibited a whole regiment of Ghosts." 'Tales of Terror' were printed at Weybridge in 1801, and two or three editions of 'Tales of Wonder', to which Byron refers, came out in the same year. Lewis borrowed so freely from all sources that the collection was called "Tales of Plunder." In the first edition (two vols., printed by W. Bulmer for the author, 1801) the first eighteen poems, with the exception of 'The Fire King' (xii.) by Walter Scott, are by Lewis, either original or translated. Scott also contributed 'Glenfinlas, The Eve of St. John, Frederick and Alice, The Wild Huntsmen (Der Wilde Jäger). Southey contributed six poems, including 'The Old Woman of Berkeley' (xxiv.). 'The Little Grey Man' (xix.) is by H. Bunbury. The second volume is made up from Burns, Gray, Parnell, Glover, Percy's 'Reliques', and other sources.

A second edition, published in 1801, which consists of thirty-two ballads (Southey's are not included), advertises "'Tales of Terror' printed uniform with this edition of 'Tales of Wonder'." 'Romantic Tales', in four volumes, appeared in 1808. Of his other works, 'The Captive, A Monodrama', was played in 1803; the 'Bravo of Venice, A Translation from the German', in 1804; and 'Timour the Tartar' in 1811. His 'Journal of a West Indian Proprietor' was not published till 1834. He sat as M.P. for Hindon (1796-1802).

He had been a favourite in society before Byron appeared on the scene, but there is no record of any intimacy or acquaintance before 1813. When Byron was living at Geneva, Lewis visited the Maison Diodati in August, 1816, on which occasion he "translated to him Goethe's 'Faust' by word of mouth," and drew up a codicil to his will, witnessed by Byron, Shelley, and Polidori, which contained certain humane provisions for the well-being of the negroes on his Jamaica estates. He also visited him at 'La Mira' in August, 1817. Byron wrote of him after his death: "He was a good man, and a clever one, but he was a bore, a damned bore—one may say. But I liked him."

To judge from his letters to his mother and other evidence (Scott's testimony, for instance), he was a kindly, well-intentioned man, but lacking in humour. When his father condemned the indecency of the 'Monk', he assured him "that he had not the slightest idea that what he was then writing could injure the principles of any human being." "He was," said Byron, "too great a bore to lie," and the plea is evidently offered in good faith. As a writer, he is memorable chiefly for his sponsorship of German literature. Scott said of him that he had the finest ear for rhythm he ever met with—finer than Byron's; and Coleridge, in a letter to Wordsworth, Jan., 1798 ('Letters of S. T. C.' (1895), i. 237), and again in 'Table Talk' for March 20, 1834, commends his verses. Certainly his ballad of "Crazy Jane," once so famous that ladies took to wearing "Crazy Jane" hats, is of the nature of poetry. (See 'Life', 349, 362, 491, etc.; 'Life and Correspondence' of M. G. Lewis (1839), i. 158, etc.; 'Life of Scott', by J. G. Lockhart (1842), pp. 80-83, 94.)]]

[Footnote 40: "For every one knows little Matt's an M.P."—See a poem to Mr. Lewis, in 'The Statesman', supposed to be written by Mr. Jekyll.

[Joseph Jekyll (d. 1837) was celebrated for his witticisms and metrical 'jeux d'esprit' which he contributed to the 'Morning Chronicle' and the 'Evening Statesman'. His election as M.P. for Calne in 1787, at the nomination of Lord Lansdowne, gave rise to 'Jekyll, A Political Eclogue' (see 'The Rottiad' (1799), pp. 219-224). He was a favourite with the Prince Regent, at whose instance he was appointed a Master in Chancery in 1815.]]

[Footnote 41: The reader, who may wish for an explanation of this, may refer to "Strangford's Camoëns," p. 127, note to p. 56, or to the last page of the 'Edinburgh Review' of Strangford's Camoëns.

[Percy Clinton Sydney Smythe, sixth Viscount Strangford (1780-1855), published 'Translations from the Portuguese by Luis de Camoens' in 1803. The note to which Byron refers is on the canzonet 'Naö sei quem assella', "Thou hast an eye of tender blue." It runs thus:

"Locks of auburn and eyes of blue have ever been dear to the sons of song.... Sterne even considers them as indicative of qualities the most amiable.... The Translator does not wish to deem ... this unfounded. He is, however, aware of the danger to which such a confession exposes him—but he flies for protection to the temple of AUREA VENUS."

It may be added that Byron's own locks were auburn, and his eyes a greyish-blue.]]

[Footnote 42: It is also to be remarked, that the things given to the public as poems of Camoëns are no more to be found in the original Portuguese, than in the Song of Solomon.]

[Footnote 43: See his various Biographies of defunct Painters, etc. [William Hayley (1745-1820) published 'The Triumphs of Temper' in 1781, and 'The Triumph of Music' in 1804. His biography of Milton appeared in 1796, of Cowper in 1803-4, of Romney in 1809. He had produced, among other plays, 'The Happy Prescription' and 'The Two Connoisseurs' in 1784. In 1808 he would be regarded as out of date, "hobbling on" behind younger rivals in the race (see

E.B., I. 923). For his life and works, see Southey's article in the 'Quarterly Review' (vol. xxxi. p. 263). The appeal to "tarts" to "spare the text," is possibly an echo of 'The Dunciad', i. 155, 156—

"Of these twelve volumes, twelve of amplest size,
Redeemed from topers and defrauded pies."

The meaning of the appeal is fixed by such a passage as this from 'The Blues', where the company discuss Wordsworth's appointment to a Collectorship of Stamps—

"'Inkle'.
I shall think of him oft when I buy a new hat;
There his works will appear.

"'Lady Bluemount'.
                Sir, they reach to the Ganges.

"'Inkle'.
I sha'n't go so far. I can have them at Grange's."

Grange's was a well-known pastry-cook's in Piccadilly. In Pierce Egan's 'Life in London' (ed. 1821), p. 70, 'note' 1, the author writes, "As I sincerely hope that this work will shrink from the touch of a pastry-cook, and also avoid the foul uses of a trunk-maker ... I feel induced now to describe, for the benefit of posterity, the pedigree of a Dandy in 1820."]

[Footnote 44: Hayley's two most notorious verse productions are 'Triumphs of Temper' and 'The Triumph of Music'. He has also written much Comedy in rhyme, Epistles, etc., etc. As he is rather an elegant writer of notes and biography, let us recommend POPE'S advice to WYCHERLEY to Mr. H.'s consideration, viz., "to convert poetry into prose," which may be easily done by taking away the final syllable of each couplet.]

[Footnote 45: Lines 319-326 do not form part of the original 'MS'. A slip of paper which contains a fair copy of the lines in Byron's handwriting has been, with other fragments, bound up with Dallas's copy of 'British Bards'. In the 'MS'. this place is taken by a passage and its pendant note, which Byron omitted at the request of Dallas, who was a friend of Pratt's:—

"In verse most stale, unprofitable, flat—
Come, let us change the scene, and "glean" with Pratt;
In him an author's luckless lot behold,
Condemned to make the books which once he sold:

Degraded man! again resume thy trade—
The votaries of the Muse are ill repaid,
Though daily puffs once more invite to buy
A new edition of thy 'Sympathy.'"

"Mr. Pratt, once a Bath bookseller, now a London author, has written as much, to as little purpose, as any of his scribbling contemporaries. Mr. P.'s 'Sympathy' is in rhyme; but his prose productions are the most voluminous."

Samuel Jackson Pratt (1749-1814), actor, itinerant lecturer, poet of the Cruscan school, tragedian, and novelist, published a large number of volumes. His 'Gleanings' in England, Holland, Wales, and Westphalia attained some reputation. His 'Sympathy; a Poem' (1788) passed through several editions. His pseudonym was Courtney Melmoth. He was a patron of the cobbler-poet, Blacket]]

[Footnote 46: Mr. Grahame has poured forth two volumes of Cant, under the name of 'Sabbath Walks' and 'Biblical Pictures'. [James Grahame (1765-1811), a lawyer, who subsequently took Holy Orders. 'The Sabbath', a poem, was published anonymously in 1804; and to a second edition were added 'Sabbath Walks'. 'Biblical Pictures' appeared in 1807.]

[Footnote 47: The Rev. W. Lisle Bowles (1768-1850). His edition of Pope's 'Works', in ten vols., which stirred Byron's gall, appeared in 1807. The 'Fall of Empires', Tyre, Carthage, etc., is the subject of part of the third book of 'The Spirit of Discovery by Sea' (1805). Lines "To a Withered Leaf," are, perhaps, of later date; but the "sear tresses" and "shivering leaves" of "Autumn's gradual gloom" are familiar images in his earlier poems. Byron's senior by twenty years, he was destined to outlive him by more than a quarter of a century; but when 'English Bards, etc.', was in progress, he was little more than middle-aged, and the "three score years" must have been written in the spirit of prophecy. As it chanced, the last word rested with him, and it was a generous one. Addressing Moore, in 1824, he says ('Childe Harold's Last Pilgrimage')—

"So Harold ends, in Greece, his pilgrimage!
There fitly ending—in that land renown'd,
Whose mighty Genius lives in Glory's page,—
He on the Muses' consecrated ground,
Sinking to rest, while his young brows are bound
With their unfading wreath!"

Among his poems are a "Sonnet to Oxford," and "Stanzas on hearing the Bells of Ostend."]

[Footnote 48: "Awake a louder," etc., is the first line in BOWLES'S 'Spirit of Discovery': a very spirited and pretty dwarf Epic. Among other exquisite lines we have the following:—

——"A kiss
Stole on the list'ning silence, never yet
Here heard; they trembled even as if the power," etc., etc.

That is, the woods of Madeira trembled to a kiss; very much astonished, as well they might be, at such a phenomenon.

"Mis-quoted and misunderstood by me; but not intentionally. It was not the 'woods,' but the people in them who trembled—why, Heaven only knows—unless they were overheard making this prodigious smack."-B., 1816.]

[Footnote 49: The episode above alluded to is the story of "Robert à Machin" and "Anna d'Arfet," a pair of constant lovers, who performed the kiss above mentioned, that startled the woods of Madeira. [See Byron's letter to Murray, Feb. 7, 1821, "On Bowies' Strictures," 'Life', p. 688.]]

[Footnote 50: CURLL is one of the Heroes of the 'Dunciad', and was a bookseller. Lord Fanny is the poetical name of Lord HERVEY, author of 'Lines to the Imitator of Horace'.]

[Footnote 51: Lord BOLINGBROKE hired MALLET to traduce POPE after his decease, because the poet had retained some copies of a work by Lord Bolingbroke—the "Patriot King,"—which that splendid, but malignant genius had ordered to be destroyed.]

[Footnote 52: Dennis the critic, and Ralph the rhymester:—

"Silence, ye Wolves! while Ralph to Cynthia howls,
Making Night hideous: answer him, ye owls!"
                    DUNCIAD.

[Book III. II. 165, 166, Pope wrote, "And makes night," etc.]]

[Footnote 53: See Bowles's late edition of Pope's works, for which he received three hundred pounds. [Twelve hundred guineas.—'British Bards'.] Thus Mr. B. has experienced how much easier it is to profit by the reputation of another, than to elevate his own. ["Too savage all this on Bowles," wrote Byron, in 1816, but he afterwards returned to his original sentiments. "Although," he says (Feb. 7, 1821), "I regret having published 'English Bards, and Scotch Reviewers', the part which I regret the least is that which regards Mr. Bowles, with reference to Pope. Whilst I was writing that publication, in 1807 and 1808, Mr. Hobhouse was desirous that I should express our mutual opinion of Pope, and of Mr. Bowles's edition of his works. As I had completed my outline, and felt lazy, I requested that 'he' would do so. He did it. His fourteen lines on Bowles's Pope are in the first edition of 'English Bards', and are quite as severe, and much more poetical, than my own, in the second. On reprinting the work, as I put my name to it, I omitted Mr. Hobhouse's lines, by which the work gained less than Mr. Bowles.... I am grieved to say that, in reading over those lines, I repent of their having so far fallen short of what I meant to express upon the subject of his edition of Pope's works" ('Life', pp. 688, 689). The lines supplied by Hobhouse are here subjoined:—

"Stick to thy sonnets, man!—at least they sell.
Or take the only path that open lies
For modern worthies who would hope to rise:
Fix on some well-known name, and, bit by bit,
Pare off the merits of his worth and wit:
On each alike employ the critic's knife,
And when a comment fails, prefix a life;
Hint certain failings, faults before unknown,
Review forgotten lies, and add your own;
Let no disease, let no misfortune 'scape,
And print, if luckily deformed, his shape:
Thus shall the world, quite undeceived at last,
Cleave to their present wits, and quit their past;
Bards once revered no more with favour view,
But give their modern sonneteers their due;
Thus with the dead may living merit cope,
Thus Bowles may triumph o'er the shade of Pope."]]

[Footnote 54:

"'Helicon' is a mountain, and not a fish-pond. It should have been 'Hippocrene.'"—B., 1816.

[The correction was made in the Fifth Edition.]]

[Footnote 55: Mr. Cottle, Amos, Joseph, I don't know which, but one or both, once sellers of books they did not write, and now writers of books they do not sell, have published a pair of Epics—'Alfred' (poor Alfred! Pye has been at him too!)—'Alfred' and the 'Fall of Cambria'.

"All right. I saw some letters of this fellow (Jh. Cottle) to an unfortunate poetess, whose productions, which the poor woman by no means thought vainly of, he attacked so roughly and bitterly, that I could hardly regret assailing him, even were it unjust, which it is not—for verily he is an ass."—B., 1816.

[Compare 'Poetry of the Anti-Jacobin'—

"And Cottle, not he whom that Alfred made famous,
But Joseph of Bristol, the brother of Amos."

The identity of the brothers Cottle appears to have been a matter beneath the notice both of the authors of the 'Anti-Jacobin' and of Byron. Amos Cottle, who died in 1800 (see Lamb's Letter to Coleridge of Oct. 9, 1800; 'Letters of C. Lamb', 1888, i. 140), was the author of a 'Translation of the Edda of Soemund', published in 1797. Joseph Cottle, 'inter alia', published 'Alfred' in 1801, and 'The Fall of Cambria', 1807. An 'Expostulatory Epistle', in which Joseph avenges Amos and solemnly castigates the author of 'Don Juan', was issued in 1819 (see Lamb's Letter to Cottle, Nov. 5, 1819), and was reprinted in the Memoir of Amos Cottle, inserted in his brother's 'Early Recollections of Coleridge' (London, 1837, i. 119). The "unfortunate poetess" was, probably, Ann Yearsley, the Bristol milk-woman. Wordsworth, too (see 'Recollections of the Table-Talk of S. Rogers', 1856, p. 235), dissuaded her from publishing her poems. Roughness and bitterness were not among Cottle's faults or foibles, and it is possible that Byron misconceived the purport of the correspondence.]]

[Footnote 56: Mr. Maurice hath manufactured the component parts of a ponderous quarto, upon the beauties of "Richmond Hill," and the like:—it also takes in a charming view of Turnham Green, Hammersmith, Brentford, Old and New, and the parts adjacent. [The Rev. Thomas Maurice (1754-1824) had this at least in common with Byron—that his 'History of Ancient and Modern Hindostan' was severely attacked in the 'Edinburgh Review'. He published a vindication of his work in 1805. He must have confined his dulness to his poems ('Richmond Hill' (1807), etc.), for his 'Memoirs' (1819) are amusing, and, though otherwise blameless, he left behind him the reputation of an "indiscriminate enjoyment" of literary and other society. Lady Anne Hamilton alludes to him in 'Epics of the Ton' (1807), p. 165—

"Or warmed like Maurice by Museum fire,
From Ganges dragged a hurdy-gurdy lyre."

He was assistant keeper of MSS. at the British Museum from 1799 till his death.]]

[Footnote 57: Poor MONTGOMERY, though praised by every English Review, has been bitterly reviled by the 'Edinburgh'. After all, the Bard of Sheffield is a man of considerable genius. His 'Wanderer of Switzerland' is worth a thousand 'Lyrical Ballads', and at least fifty 'Degraded Epics'.

[James Montgomery (1771-1854) was born in Ayrshire, but settled at Sheffield, where he edited a newspaper, the 'Iris', a radical print, which brought him into conflict with the authorities. His early poems were held up to ridicule in the 'Edinburgh Review' by Jeffrey, in Jan. 1807. It was probably the following passage which provoked Byron's note: "When every day is bringing forth some new work from the pen of Scott, Campbell,... Wordsworth, and Southey, it is natural to feel some disgust at the undistinguishing voracity which can swallow down these... verses to a pillow." The 'Wanderer of Switzerland', which Byron said he preferred to the 'Lyrical Ballads', was published in 1806. The allusion in line 419 is to the first stanza of 'The Lyre'—

"Where the roving rill meand'red
Down the green, retiring vale,
Poor, forlorn Alæcus wandered,
Pale with thoughts—serenely pale."

He is remembered chiefly as the writer of some admirable hymns. ('Vide ante', p. 107, "Answer to a Beautiful Poem," and 'note'.)]

[Footnote 58: Arthur's Seat; the hill which overhangs Edinburgh.]

[Footnote 59: Lines 439-527 are not in the 'MS.' The first draft of the passage on Jeffrey, which appears to have found a place in 'British Bards' and to have been afterwards cut out, runs as follows:—

"Who has not heard in this enlightened age,
When all can criticise the historic page,
Who has not heard in James's Bigot Reign
Of Jefferies! monarch of the scourge, and chain,
Jefferies the wretch whose pestilential breath,
Like the dread Simoom, winged the shaft of Death;

The old, the young to Fate remorseless gave
Nor spared one victim from the common grave?

"Such was the Judge of James's iron time,
When Law was Murder, Mercy was a crime,
Till from his throne by weary millions hurled
The Despot roamed in Exile through the world.

"Years have rolled on;—in all the lists of Shame,
Who now can parallel a Jefferies' name?
With hand less mighty, but with heart as black
With voice as willing to decree the Rack,
With tongue envenomed, with intentions foul
The same in name and character and soul."

The first four lines of the above, which have been erased, are to be found on p. 16 of 'British Bards.' Pages 17, 18, are wanting, and quarto proofs of lines 438-527 have been inserted. Lines 528-539 appear for the first time in the Fifth Edition.]]

[Footnote 60: "Too ferocious—this is mere insanity."—B., 1816. [The comment applies to lines 432-453.]]

[Footnote 61: "All this is bad, because personal."—B., 1816.]

[Footnote 62: In 1806, Messrs. Jeffrey and Moore met at Chalk Farm. The duel was prevented by the interference of the Magistracy; and on examination, the balls of the pistols were found to have evaporated. This incident gave occasion to much waggery in the daily prints. [The first four editions read, "the balls of the pistols, like the courage of the combatants."]

[The following disclaimer to the foregoing note appears in the MS. in Leigh Hunt's copy of the Fourth Edition, 1811. It was first printed in the Fifth Edition:—]

"I am informed that Mr. Moore published at the time a disavowal of the statements in the newspapers, as far as regarded himself; and, in justice to him, I mention this circumstance. As I never heard of it before, I cannot state the particulars, and was only made acquainted with the fact very lately. November 4, 1811."

[As a matter of fact, it was Jeffrey's pistol that was found to be leadless.]]

[Footnote 63: The Tweed here behaved with proper decorum; it would have been highly reprehensible in the English half of the river to have shown the smallest symptom of apprehension.]

[Footnote 64: This display of sympathy on the part of the Tolbooth (the principal prison in Edinburgh), which truly seems to have been most affected on this occasion, is much to be commended. It was to be apprehended, that the many unhappy criminals executed in the front might have rendered the Edifice more callous. She is said to be of the softer sex, because her delicacy of feeling on this day was truly feminine, though, like most feminine impulses, perhaps a little selfish.]

[Footnote 65: Line 508. For "oat-fed phalanx," the Quarto Proof and Editions 1-4 read "ranks illustrious." The correction is made in 'MS'. in the Annotated Edition. It was suggested that the motto of the 'Edinburgh Review' should have been, "Musam tenui meditamur avenâ."]

[Footnote 66: His Lordship has been much abroad, is a member of the Athenian Society, and reviewer of Gell's 'Topography of Troy'. [George Gordon, fourth Earl of Aberdeen (1784-1860), published in 1822 'An Inquiry into the Principles of Beauty in Grecian Architecture'. His grandfather purchased Gight, the property which Mrs. Byron had sold to pay her husband's debts. This may have been an additional reason for the introduction of his name.]]

[Footnote 67: Mr. Herbert is a translator of Icelandic and other poetry. One of the principal pieces is a 'Song on the Recovery of Thor's Hammer': the translation is a pleasant chant in the vulgar tongue, and endeth thus:—

"Instead of money and rings, I wot,
The hammer's bruises were her lot.
Thus Odin's son his hammer got."

[William Herbert (1778-1847), son of the first Earl of Carnarvon, edited 'Musæ Etonenses' in 1795, whilst he was still at school. He was one of the earliest contributors to the 'Edinburgh Review'. At the time when Byron was writing his satire, he was M.P. for Hampshire, but in 1814 he took Orders. He was appointed Dean of Manchester in 1840, and republished his poetical works, and among them his Icelandic Translations or 'Horæ Scandicæ (Miscellaneous Works', 2 vols.), in 1842.]]

[Footnote 68: The Rev. SYDNEY SMITH, the reputed Author of 'Peter Plymley's Letters', and sundry criticisms. [Sydney Smith (1771-1845), the "witty Canon of St. Paul's," was one of the founders, and for a short time (1802) the editor, of the 'Edinburgh Review'. His 'Letters on the Catholicks, from Peter Plymley to his brother Abraham', appeared in 1807-8.]

[Footnote 69: Mr. HALLAM reviewed PAYNE KNIGHT'S "Taste," and was exceedingly severe on some Greek verses therein. It was not discovered that the lines were Pindar's till the press rendered it impossible to cancel the critique, which still stands an everlasting monument of Hallam's ingenuity.—['Note added to Second Edition':

Hallam is incensed because he is falsely accused, seeing that he never dineth at Holland House. If this be true, I am sorry—not for having said so, but on his account, as I understand his Lordship's feasts are preferable to his compositions. If he did not review Lord HOLLAND'S performance, I am glad; because it must have been painful to read, and irksome to praise it. If Mr. HALLAM will tell me who did review it, the real name shall find a place in the text; provided, nevertheless, the said name be of two orthodox musical syllables, and will come into the verse: till then, HALLAM must stand for want of a better.]

[Henry Hallam (1777-1859), author of 'Europe during the Middle Ages', 1808, etc.

"This," said Byron, "is the style in which history ought to be
written, if it is wished to impress it on the memory"

('Lady Blessington's Conversations with Lord Byron', 1834, p. 213). The article in question was written by Dr. John Allen, Lord Holland's domestic physician, and Byron was misled by the similarity of sound in the two names (see H. C. Robinson's 'Diary', i. 277), or repeated what Hodgson had told him (see Introduction, and Letter 102, 'note' i).

For a disproof that Hallam wrote the article, see 'Gent. Mag'., 1830, pt. i. p. 389; and for an allusion to the mistake in the review, compare 'All the Talents', p. 96, and 'note'.

"Spare me not 'Chronicles' and 'Sunday News',
Spare me not 'Pamphleteers' and 'Scotch Reviews'"

"The best literary joke I recollect is its [the 'Edin. Rev'.] attempting to prove some of the Grecian Pindar rank non sense, supposing it to have been written by Mr. P. Knight."]

[Footnote 70: Pillans is a [private, 'MS'.] tutor at Eton. [James Pillans (1778-1864), Rector of the High School, and Professor of Humanity in the University, Edinburgh. Byron probably assumed that the

review of Hodgson's 'Translation of Juvenal', in the 'Edinburgh Review',
April, 1808, was by him.]]

Footnote 71: The Honourable G. Lambe reviewed "BERESFORD'S Miseries," and is moreover Author of a farce enacted with much applause at the Priory, Stanmore; and damned with great expedition at the late theatre, Covent Garden. It was entitled 'Whistle for It'. [See note, 'supra', on line 57.] His review of James Beresford's 'Miseries of Human Life; or the Last Groans of Timothy Testy and Samuel Sensitive', appeared in the 'Edinburgh Review 'for Oct. 1806.]

[Footnote: 72: Mr. Brougham, in No. XXV. of the 'Edinburgh Review', throughout the article concerning Don Pedro de Cevallos, has displayed more politics than policy; many of the worthy burgesses of Edinburgh being so incensed at the infamous principles it evinces, as to have withdrawn their subscriptions.—[Here followed, in the First Edition: "The name of this personage is pronounced Broom in the south, but the truly northern and 'musical' pronunciation is BROUGH-AM, in two syllables;" but for this, Byron substituted in the Second Edition: "It seems that Mr. Brougham is not a Pict, as I supposed, but a Borderer, and his name is pronounced Broom, from Trent to Tay:—so be it."

The title of the work was "Exposition of the Practices and Machinations which led to the usurpation of the Crown of Spain, and the means adopted by the Emperor of the French to carry it into execution," by Don Pedro Cevallos. The article, which appeared in Oct. 1808, was the joint composition of Jeffrey and Brougham, and proved a turning-point in the political development of the 'Review'.]]

[Footnote 73: I ought to apologise to the worthy Deities for introducing a new Goddess with short petticoats to their notice: but, alas! what was to be done? I could not say Caledonia's Genius, it being well known there is no genius to be found from Clackmannan to Caithness; yet without supernatural agency, how was Jeffrey to be saved? The national "Kelpies" are too unpoetical, and the "Brownies" and "gude neighbours" (spirits of a good disposition) refused to extricate him. A Goddess, therefore, has been called for the purpose; and great ought to be the gratitude of Jeffrey, seeing it is the only communication he ever held, or is likely to hold, with anything heavenly.]

[Footnote 74: Lines 528-539 appeared for the first time in the Fifth Edition.]

[Footnote 75: See the colour of the back binding of the 'Edinburgh Review'.]

[Footnote 76: "Bad enough, and on mistaken grounds too."—B., 1816. [The comment applies to the whole passage on Lord Holland.]

[Henry Richard Vassall, third Lord Holland (1773-1840), to whom Byron dedicated the 'Bride of Abydos' (1813). His 'Life of Lope de Vega' (see note 4) was published in 1806, and 'Three Comedies from the Spanish', in 1807.]]

[Footnote 77: Henry Petty (1780-1863) succeeded his brother as third Marquis of Lansdowne in 1809. He was a regular attendant at the social and political gatherings of his relative, Lord Holland; and as Holland House was regarded as one of the main rallying-points of the Whig party and of the Edinburgh Reviewers, the words, "whipper-in and hunts-man," probably refer to their exertions in this respect.]

[Footnote 78: See note 1, p. 337. (Footnote 69—Text Ed.)]

[Footnote 79: Lord Holland has translated some specimens of Lope de Vega, inserted in his life of the author. Both are bepraised by his 'disinterested' guests.]

[Footnote 80: Certain it is, her ladyship is suspected of having displayed her matchless wit in the 'Edinburgh Review'. However that may be, we know from good authority, that the manuscripts are submitted to her perusal—no doubt, for correction.]

[Footnote 81: In the melo-drama of 'Tekeli', that heroic prince is clapt into a barrel on the stage; a new asylum for distressed heroes.—[In the 'MS'. and 'British Bards' the note stands thus:—"In the melodrama of 'Tekeli', that heroic prince is clapt into a barrel on the stage, and Count Everard in the fortress hides himself in a green-house built expressly for the occasion. 'Tis a pity that Theodore Hook, who is really a man of talent, should confine his genius to such paltry productions as 'The Fortress, Music Mad', etc. etc." Theodore Hook (1788-1841) produced 'Tekeli' in 1806. 'Fortress' and 'Music Mad' were played in 1807. He had written some eight or ten popular plays before he was twenty-one.]]

[Footnote 82: 'Vide post', 1. 591, note 3.]

[Footnote 83: William Henry West Betty (1791-1874) ("the Young Roscius") made his first appearance on the London stage as Selim, disguised as Achmet, in 'Barbarossa', Dec. 1, 1804, and his last, as a boy actor, in 'Tancred', and Captain Flash in 'Miss in her Teens', Mar. 17, 1806, but acted in the provinces till 1808. So great was the excitement on the occasion of his 'début', that the military were held in readiness to assist in keeping order. Having made a large fortune, he finally retired from the stage in 1824, and passed the last fifty years of his life in retirement, surviving his fame by more than half a century.]

[Footnote 84: All these are favourite expressions of Mr. Reynolds, and prominent in his comedies, living and defunct. [Frederick Reynolds (1764-1841) produced nearly one hundred plays, one of the most successful of which was 'The Caravan, or the Driver and his Dog'. The text alludes to his endeavour to introduce the language of ordinary life on the stage. Compare 'The Children of Apollo', p. 9—

"But in his diction Reynolds grossly errs;
For whether the love hero smiles or mourns,
'Tis oh! and ah! and ah! and oh! by turns."]]

[Footnote 85: James Kenney (1780-1849). Among his very numerous plays, the most successful were 'Raising the Wind' (1803), and 'Sweethearts and Wives' (1823). 'The World' was brought out at Covent Garden, March 30, 1808, and had a considerable run. He was intimate with Charles and Mary Lamb (see 'Letters of Charles Lamb', ii. 16, 44).]

[Footnote 85a: Mr. T. Sheridan, the new Manager of Drury Lane theatre, stripped the Tragedy of 'Bonduca' ['Caratach' in the original 'MS'.] of the dialogue, and exhibited the scenes as the spectacle of 'Caractacus'. Was this worthy of his sire? or of himself? [Thomas Sheridan (1775-1817), most famous as the son of Richard Brinsley Sheridan, and father of Lady Dufferin, Mrs. Norton, and the Duchess of Somerset, was author of several plays. His 'Bonduca' was played at Covent Garden, May 3, 1808. The following answer to a real or fictitious correspondent, in the 'European Magazine' for May, 1808, is an indication of contemporary opinion: "The Fishwoman's letter to the author of 'Caractacus' on the art of gutting is inadmissible." For anecdotes of Thomas Sheridan, see Angelo's 'Reminiscences', 1828, ii. 170-175. See, too, 'Epics of the Ton', p. 264.]]

[Footnote 86: George Colman, the younger (1762-1836), wrote numerous dramas, several of which, 'e.g. The Iron Chest' (1796), 'John Bull' (1803), 'The Heir-at-Law' (1808), have been popular with more than one generation of playgoers. An amusing companion, and a favourite at Court, he was appointed Lieutenant of the Yeomen of the Guard, and examiner of plays by Royal favour, but his reckless mode of life kept him always in difficulties. 'John Bull' is referred to in 'Hints from Horace', line 166.]]

[Footnote 87: Richard Cumberland (1732-1811), the original of Sir Fretful Plagiary in 'The Critic', a man of varied abilities, wrote poetry, plays, novels, classical translations, and works of religious controversy. He was successively Fellow of Trinity College, Cambridge, secretary to the Lord Lieutenant of Ireland, and secretary to the Board of Trade. His best known plays are 'The West Indian, The Wheels of Fortune', and 'The Jew'. He published his 'Memoirs' in 1806-7.]]

[Footnote 88: Sheridan's translation of 'Pizarro', by Kotzebue, was first played at Drury Lane, 1799. Southey wrote of it, "It is impossible to sink below 'Pizarro'. Kotzebue's play might have passed for the worst possible if Sheridan had not proved the possibility of making it worse" (Southey's 'Letters', i. 87). Gifford alludes to it in a note to 'The Mæviad' as "the translation so maliciously attributed to Sheridan."]

[Footnote 89: In all editions, previous to the fifth, it was, "Kemble lives to tread." Byron used to say, that, of actors, "Cooke was the most natural, Kemble the most supernatural, Kean the medium between the two; but that Mrs. Siddons was worth them all put together." Such effect, however, had Kean's acting on his mind, that once, on seeing him play Sir Giles Overreach, he was seized with a fit.]

[Footnote 90: See 'supra', line 562.]

[Footnote 91: Andrew Cherry (1762-1812) acted many parts in Ireland and in the provinces, and for a few years appeared at Drury Lane. He was popular in Dublin, where he was known as "Little Cherry." He was painted as Lazarillo in Jephson's 'Two Strings to Your Bow'. He wrote 'The Travellers' (1806), 'Peter the Great' (1807), and other plays.]]

[Footnote 92: Mr. [now Sir Lumley] Skeffington is the illustrious author of 'The Sleeping Beauty;' and some comedies, particularly 'Maids and Bachelors: Baccalaurii' baculo magis quam lauro digni.

[Lumley St. George (afterwards Sir Lumley) Skeffington (1768-1850). Besides the plays mentioned in the note, he wrote 'The Maid of Honour' (1803) and 'The Mysterious Bride' (1808). 'Amatory Verses, by Tom Shuffleton of the Middle Temple' (1815), are attributed to his pen. They are prefaced by a dedicatory letter to Byron, which includes a coarse but clever skit in the style of 'English Bards'. "Great Skeffington" was a great dandy. According to Capt. Gronow ('Reminiscences', i. 63), "he used to paint his face so that he looked like a French toy; he dressed 'à la Robespierre', and practised all the follies;... was remarkable for his politeness and courtly manners... You always knew of his approach by an 'avant courier' of sweet smell." His play 'The Sleeping Beauty' had a considerable vogue.]]

[Footnote 93: Thomas John Dibdin (1771-1841), natural son of Charles Dibdin the elder, made his first appearance on the stage at the age of four, playing Cupid to Mrs. Siddons' Venus at the Shakespearian Jubilee in 1775. One of his best known pieces is 'The Jew and the Doctor' (1798). His pantomime, 'Mother Goose', in which Grimaldi took a part, was played at Covent Garden in 1807, and is said to have brought the management £20,000.]

[Footnote 94: Mr. Greenwood is, we believe, scene-painter to Drury Lane theatre—as such, Mr. Skeffington is much indebted to him.]

[Footnote 95: Naldi and Catalani require little notice; for the visage of the one, and the salary of the other, will enable us long to recollect these amusing vagabonds. Besides, we are still black and blue from the squeeze on the first night of the Lady's appearance in trousers. [Guiseppe Naldi (1770-1820) made his 'début' on the London stage at the King's Theatre in April, 1806. In conjunction with Catalani and Braham, he gave concerts at Willis' Rooms. Angelica Catalani (circ. 1785-1849), a famous soprano, Italian by birth and training, made her 'début' at Venice in 1795. She remained in England for eight years (1806-14). Her first appearance in England was at the King's Theatre, in Portogallo's 'Semiramide,' in 1806. Her large salary was one of the causes which provoked the O. P. (Old Prices) Riots in December, 1809, at Covent Garden. Praed says of his 'Ball Room Belle'—

"She warbled Handel: it was grand;
She made the Catalani jealous."]

[Footnote 96: Moore says that the following twenty lines were struck off one night after Lord Byron's return from the Opera, and sent the next morning to the printer. The date of the letter to Dallas, with which the lines were enclosed, suggests that the representation which provoked the outburst was that of 'I Villegiatori Rezzani,' at the King's Theatre, February 21, 1809. The first piece, in which Naldi and Catalani were the principal singers, was followed by d'Egville's musical extravaganza, 'Don Quichotte, on les Noces de Gamache.' In the 'corps de ballet' were Deshayes, for many years master of the 'ballet' at the King's Theatre; Miss Gayton, who had played a Sylph at Drury Lane as early as 1806 (she was married, March 18, 1809, to the Rev. William Murray, brother of Sir James Pulteney, Bart.—'Morning Chronicle,' December 30, 1810), and Mademoiselle Angiolini, "elegant of figure, 'petite', but finely formed, with the manner of Vestris." Mademoiselle Presle does not seem to have taken part in 'Don Quichotte;'

but she was well known as 'première danseuse' in 'La Belle Laitière, La Fête Chinoise,' and other ballets.]]

[Footnote 97: For "whet" Editions 1-5 read "raise." Lines 632-637 are marked "good" in the Annotated Fourth Edition.]

[Footnote 98: To prevent any blunder, such as mistaking a street for a man, I beg leave to state, that it is the institution, and not the Duke of that name, which is here alluded to.

A gentleman, with whom I am slightly acquainted, lost in the Argyle Rooms several thousand pounds at Backgammon.[A] It is but justice to the manager in this instance to say, that some degree of disapprobation was manifested: but why are the implements of gaming allowed in a place devoted to the society of both sexes? A pleasant thing for the wives and daughters of those who are blessed or cursed with such connections, to hear the Billiard-Balls rattling in one room, and the dice in another! That this is the case I myself can testify, as a late unworthy member of an Institution which materially affects the morals of the higher orders, while the lower may not even move to the sound of a tabor and fiddle, without a chance of indictment for riotous behaviour. [The Argyle Institution, founded by Colonel Greville, flourished many years before the Argyll Rooms were built by Nash in 1818. This mention of Greville's name caused him to demand an explanation from Byron, but the matter was amicably settled by Moore and G. F. Leckie, who acted on behalf of the disputants (see 'Life', pp. 160, 161).]]

[Sub-Footnote A: "True. It was Billy Way who lost the money. I knew him, and was a subscriber to the Argyle at the time of this event."—B., 1816.]

[Footnote 99: Petronius, "Arbiter elegantiarum" to Nero, "and a very pretty fellow in his day," as Mr. Congreve's "Old Bachelor" saith of Hannibal.]

[Footnote 100: "We are authorised to state that Mr. Greville, who has a small party at his private assembly rooms at the Argyle, will receive from 10 to 12 [p.m.] masks who have Mrs. Chichester's Institution tickets.—Morning Post, June 7, 1809.]

[Footnote 101: See note on line 686, infra.]

[Footnote 102: 'Clodius'—"Mutato nomine de te Fabula narratur."—['MS'] [The allusion is to the well-known incidents of his intrigue with Pompeia, Cæsar's wife, and his sacrilegious intrusion into the mysteries of the Bona Dea. The Romans had a proverb, "Clodius accuset Moechos?" (Juv., 'Sat.' ii. 27). That "Steenie" should lecture on the "turpitude of incontinence!" ('The Fortunes of Nigel,' cap. xxxii.)]]

[Footnote 103: I knew the late Lord Falkland well. On Sunday night I beheld him presiding at his own table, in all the honest pride of hospitality; on Wednesday morning, at three o'clock, I saw stretched before me all that remained of courage, feeling, and a host of passions. He was a gallant and successful officer: his faults were the faults of a sailor—as such, Britons will forgive them. ["His behaviour on the field was worthy of a better fate, and his conduct on the bed of death evinced all the firmness of a man without the farce of repentance—I say the farce of repentance, for death-bed repentance is a farce, and as little serviceable to the soul at such a moment as the surgeon to the body, though both may be useful if taken in time. Some hireling in the papers forged a tale about an agonized voice, etc. On mentioning the circumstance to Mr. Heaviside, he exclaimed, 'Good God! what absurdity to talk in this manner of one who died like a lion!'—he did more."—'MS'] He died like a brave man in a better cause; for had he fallen in like manner on the deck of the frigate to which he was just appointed, his last moments would have been held up by his countrymen as an example to succeeding heroes.

[Charles John Carey, ninth Viscount Falkland, died from a wound received in a duel with Mr. A. Powell on Feb. 28, 1809. (See Byron's letter to his mother, March 6, 1809.) The story of "the agonized voice" may be traced to a paragraph in the 'Morning Post,' March 2, 1809: "Lord Falkland, after hearing the surgeon's opinion, said with a faltering voice and as intelligibly as the agonized state of his body and mind permitted, "I acquit Mr. Powell of all blame; in this transaction I alone am culpable."']]

[Footnote 104: "Yes: and a precious chase they led me."—B., 1816.]

[Footnote 105: "'Fool' enough, certainly, then, and no wiser since."—B., 1816.]

[Footnote 106: What would be the sentiments of the Persian Anacreon, HAFIZ, could he rise from his splendid sepulchre at Sheeraz (where he reposes with FERDOUSI and SADI, the Oriental Homer and Catullus), and behold his name assumed by one STOTT of DROMORE, the most impudent and execrable of literary poachers for the Daily Prints?]

[Footnote 107: Miles Peter Andrews (d. 1824) was the owner of large powder-mills at Dartford. He was M.P. for Bewdley. He held a good social position, but his intimate friends were actors and playwrights. His 'Better Late than Never' (which Reynolds and Topham helped him to write) was played for the first time at Drury Lane, October 17, 1790, with Kemble as Saville, and

Mrs. Jordan as Augusta. He is mentioned in 'The Baviad', l. 10; and in a note Gifford satirizes his prologue to 'Lorenzo', and describes him as an "industrious paragraph-monger."]]

[Footnote 108: In a manuscript fragment, bound in the same volume as 'British Bards', we find these lines:—

"In these, our times, with daily wonders big,
A Lettered peer is like a lettered pig;
Both know their Alphabet, but who, from thence,
Infers that peers or pigs have manly sense?
Still less that such should woo the graceful nine;
Parnassus was not made for lords and swine."]

[Footnote 109: Wentworth Dillon, 4th Earl of Roscommon (1634-1685), author of many translations and minor poems, endeavoured (circ. 1663) to found an English literary academy.]

[Footnote 110: John Sheffield, Earl of Mulgrave (1658), Marquis of Normanby (1694), Duke of Buckingham (1703) (1649-1721), wrote an 'Essay upon Poetry', and several other works.]

[Footnote 111: Lines 727-740 were added after 'British Bards' had been printed, and are included in the First Edition, but the appearance in 'British Bards' of lines 723-726 and 741-746, which have been cut out from Mr. Murray's MS., forms one of many proofs as to the identity of the text of the 'MS'. and the printed Quarto.]]

[Footnote 112: Frederick Howard, 5th Earl of Carlisle, K.G. (1748-1825), Viceroy of Ireland, 1780-1782, and Privy Seal, etc., published 'Tragedies and Poems', 1801. He was Byron's first cousin once removed, and his guardian. 'Poems Original and Translated,' were dedicated to Lord Carlisle, and, as an erased MS. addition to 'British Bards' testifies, he was to have been excepted from the roll of titled poetasters—

"Ah, who would take their titles from their rhymes?
On 'one' alone Apollo deigns to smile,
And crowns a new Roscommon in Carlisle."

Before, however, the revised Satire was sent to the press, Carlisle ignored his cousin's request to introduce him on taking his seat in the House of Lords, and, to avenge the slight, eighteen lines of castigation supplanted the flattering couplet. Lord Carlisle suffered from a nervous disorder, and Byron was informed that some readers had scented an allusion in the words "paralytic puling." "I thank Heaven," he exclaimed, "I did not know it; and would not, could not, if I had. I must naturally be the last person to be pointed on defects or maladies."

In 1814 he consulted Rogers on the chance of conciliating Carlisle, and in 'Childe Harold', iii. 29, he laments the loss of the "young and gallant Howard" (Carlisle's youngest son) at Waterloo, and admits that "he did his sire some wrong." But, according to Medwin ('Conversations', 1824, p. 362), who prints an excellent parody on Carlisle's lines addressed to Lady Holland in 1822, in which he urges her to decline the legacy of Napoleon's snuff-box, Byron made fun of his "noble relative" to the end of the chapter ('vide post', p. 370, 'note' 2).]]

[Footnote 113: The Earl of Carlisle has lately published an eighteen-penny pamphlet on the state of the Stage, and offers his plan for building a new theatre. It is to be hoped his Lordship will be permitted to bring forward anything for the Stage—except his own tragedies. [This pamphlet was entitled 'Thoughts upon the present condition of the stage, and upon the construction of a new Theatre', anon. 1808.]

Line 732. None of the earlier editions, including the fifth and Murray, 1831, insert "and" between "petit-maître" and "pamphleteer." No doubt Byron sounded the final syllable of "maître," 'anglicé' "mailer."]]

[Footnote 114:

"Doff that lion's hide,
And hang a calf-skin on those recreant limbs."

SHAKESPEARE, 'King John.'

Lord Carlisle's works, most resplendently bound, form a conspicuous ornament to his book-shelves:—

"The rest is all but [only, MS.] leather and prunella."

"Wrong also—the provocation was not sufficient to justify such acerbity."—B., 1816.]

[Footnote 115: 'All the Blocks, or an Antidote to "All the Talents"' by Flagellum (W. H. Ireland), London, 1807: 'The Groan of the Talents, or Private Sentiments on Public Occasions,' 1807; "Gr—vile Agonistes, 'A Dramatic Poem, 1807,' etc., etc."]

[Footnote 116: "MELVILLE'S Mantle," a parody on 'Elijah's Mantle,' a poem. ['Elijah's Mantle, being verses occasioned by the death of that illustrious statesman, the Right Hon. W. Pitt.' Dedicated to the Right Rev. the Lord Bishop of Lincoln (1807), was written by James Sayer. 'Melville's Mantle, being a Parody on the poem entitled "Elijah's Mantle"' was published by Budd, 1807. 'A Monody on the death of the R. H. C. J. Fox,' by Richard Payne Knight, was printed for J. Payne, 1806-7. Another "Monody," 'Lines written on returning from the Funeral of the R. H. C. J. Fox, Friday Oct'. 10, 1806, addressed to Lord Holland, was by M. G. Lewis, and there were others.]]

[Footnote 117: This lovely little Jessica, the daughter of the noted Jew King, seems to be a follower of the Della Crusca school, and has published two volumes of very respectable absurdities in rhyme, as times go; besides sundry novels in the style of the first edition of 'The Monk.'

"She since married the 'Morning Post'—an exceeding good match; and is now dead—which is better."—B., 1816. [The last seven words are in pencil, and, possibly, by another hand. The novelist "Rosa," the daughter of "Jew King," the lordly money-lender who lived in Clarges Street, and drove a yellow chariot, may possibly be confounded with "Rosa Matilda," Mrs. Byrne (Gronow, 'Rem.' (1889), i. 132-136). (See note 1, p. 358.)]

[Footnote 118: Lines 759, 760 were added for the first time in the Fourth Edition.]

[Footnote 119: Lines 756-764, with variant ii., refer to the Della Cruscan school, attacked by Gifford in 'The Baviad' and 'The Mæviad.' Robert Merry (1755-1798), together with Mrs. Piozzi, Bertie Greatheed, William Parsons, and some Italian friends, formed a literary society called the 'Oziosi' at Florence, where they published 'The Arno Miscellany' (1784) and 'The Florence Miscellany' (1785), consisting of verses in which the authors "say kind things of each other" (Preface to 'The Florence Miscellany,' by Mrs. Piozzi). In 1787 Merry, who had become a member of the Della Cruscan Academy at Florence, returned to London, and wrote in the 'World' (then edited by Captain Topham) a sonnet on "Love," under the signature of "Della Crusca." He was answered by Mrs. Hannah Cowley, 'née' Parkhouse (1743-1809), famous as the authoress of 'The Belles Stratagem' (acted at Covent Garden in 1782), in a sonnet called "The Pen," signed "Anna Matilda." The poetical correspondence which followed was published in 'The British Album' (1789, 2 vols.) by John Bell. Other writers connected with the Della Cruscan school were "Perdita" Robinson, 'née' Darby (1758-1800), who published 'The Mistletoe' (1800) under the pseudonym "Laura Maria," and to whom Merry addressed a poem quoted by Gifford in 'The Baviad' ('note' to line 284); Charlotte Dacre, who married Byrne, Robinson's successor as editor of the 'Morning Post,' wrote under the pseudonym of "Rosa Matilda," and published poems ('Hours of Solitude,' 1805) and numerous novels ('Confessions of the Nun of St. Omer's,' 1805; 'Zofloya;' 'The Libertine,' etc.); and "Hafiz" (Robert Stott, of the 'Morning Post'). Of these writers, "Della Crusca" Merry, and "Laura Maria" Robinson, were dead; "Anna Matilda" Cowley, "Hafiz" Stott, and "Rosa Matilda" Dacre were still living. John Bell (1745-1831), the publisher of 'The British Album,' was also one of the proprietors of the 'Morning Post,' the 'Oracle,' and the 'World,' in all of which the Della Cruscans wrote. His "Owls and Nightingales" are explained by a reference to 'The Baviad' (l. 284), where Gifford pretends to mistake the nightingale, to which Merry ("Arno") addressed some lines, for an owl. "On looking again, I find the owl to be a nightingale!—N'importe."]]

[Footnote 120: These are the signatures of various worthies who figure in the poetical departments of the newspapers.]

[Footnote 121: "This was meant for poor Blackett, who was then patronised by A. I. B." (Lady Byron); "but 'that' I did not know, or this would not have been written, at least I think not."—B., 1816.

[Joseph Blacket (1786-1810), said by Southey ('Letters,' i. 172) to possess "force and rapidity," and to be endowed with "more powers than Robert Bloomfield, and an intellect of higher pitch," was the son of a labourer, and by trade a cobbler. He was brought into notice by S. J. Pratt (who published Blacket's 'Remains' in 1811), and was befriended by the Milbanke family. Miss Milbanke, afterwards Lady Byron, wrote (Sept. 2, 1809), "Seaham is at present the residence of a poet, by name Joseph Blacket, one of the Burns-like and Dermody kind, whose genius is his sole possession. I was yesterday in his company for the first time, and was much pleased with his manners and conversation. He is extremely diffident, his deportment is mild, and his countenance animated melancholy and of a satirical turn. His poems certainly display a superior genius and an enlarged mind...." Blacket died on the Seaham estate in Sept., 1810, at the age of twenty-three. (See Byron's letter to Dallas, June 28, 1811; his 'Epitaph for Joseph Blackett;' and 'Hints from Horace,' l. 734.)]]

[Footnote 122: Capel Lofft, Esq., the Mæcenas of shoemakers, and
Preface-writer-General to distressed versemen; a kind of gratis
Accoucheur to those who wish to be delivered of rhyme, but do not know
how to bring it forth.

[Capel Lofft (1751-1824), jurist, poet, critic, and horticulturist, honoured himself by his kindly patronage of Robert Bloomfield (1766-1823), who was born at Honington, near Lofft's estate of

Throston, Suffolk. Robert Bloomfield was brought up by his elder brothers— Nathaniel a tailor, and George a shoemaker. It was in the latter's workshop that he composed 'The Farmer's Boy,' which was published (1798) with the help of Lofft. He also wrote 'Rural Tales' (1802), 'Good Tidings; or News from the Farm '(1804), 'The Banks of the Wye' (1811), etc. (See 'Hints from Horace,' line 734, notes 1 and 2.)]]

[Footnote 123: See Nathaniel Bloomfield's ode, elegy, or whatever he or any one else chooses to call it, on the enclosures of "Honington Green." [Nathaniel Bloomfield, as a matter of fact, called it a ballad.—'Poems' (1803).]]

[Footnote 124: Vide 'Recollections of a Weaver in the Moorlands of Staffordshire'. [The exact title is 'The Moorland Bard; or Poetical Recollections of a Weaver', etc. 2 vols., 1807. The author was T. Bakewell, who also wrote 'A Domestic Guide to Insanity', 1805.]]

[Footnote 125: It would be superfluous to recall to the mind of the reader the authors of 'The Pleasures of Memory' and 'The Pleasures of Hope', the most beautiful didactic poems in our language, if we except Pope's 'Essay on Man': but so many poetasters have started up, that even the names of Campbell and Rogers are become strange.—[Beneath this note Byron scribbled, in 1816,—

"Pretty Miss Jaqueline
Had a nose aquiline,
And would assert rude
Things of Miss Gertrude,
While Mr. Marmion
Led a great army on,
Making Kehama look
Like a fierce Mameluke."

"I have been reading," he says, in 1813, "'Memory' again, and 'Hope' together, and retain all my preference of the former. His elegance is really wonderful—there is no such a thing as a vulgar line in his book." In the annotations of 1816, Byron remarks, "Rogers has not fulfilled the promise of his first poems, but has still very great merit."]

[Footnote 126: GIFFORD, author of the 'Baviad' and 'Mæviad', the first satires of the day, and translator of Juvenal, [and one (though not the best) of the translators of Juvenal.—'British Bards'.]]

[Footnote 127: SOTHEBY, translator of WIELAND'S 'Oberon' and Virgil's 'Georgics', and author of 'Saul', an epic poem. [William Sotheby (1757-1833) began life as a cavalry officer, but being a man of fortune, sold out of the army and devoted himself to literature, and to the patronage of men of letters. His translation of the 'Oberon' appeared in 1798, and of the 'Georgics' in 1800. 'Saul' was published in 1807. When Byron was in Venice, he conceived a dislike to Sotheby, in the belief that he had made an anonymous attack on some of his works; but, later, his verdict was, "a good man, rhymes well (if not wisely); but is a bore" ('Diary', 1821; 'Works', p. 509, note). He is "the solemn antique man of rhyme" ('Beppo', st. lxiii.), and the "Botherby" of 'The Blues'; and in 'Don Juan', Canto I. st. cxvi., we read—

"Thou shalt not covet Mr. Sotheby's house
His Pegasus nor anything that's his."]]

[Footnote 128: MACNEIL, whose poems are deservedly popular, particularly "SCOTLAND'S Scaith," and the "Waes of War," of which ten thousand copies were sold in one month. [Hector Macneil (1746-1816) wrote in defence of slavery in Jamaica, and was the author of several poems: 'Scotland's Skaith, or the History of Will and Jean' (1795), 'The Waes of War, or the Upshot of the History of Will and Jean' (1796), etc., etc.]]

[Footnote 129: Mr. GIFFORD promised publicly that the 'Baviad' and 'Mæviad' should not be his last original works: let him remember, "Mox in reluctantes dracones." [Cf. 'New Morality,' lines 29-42.]]

[Footnote 130: Henry Kirke White died at Cambridge, in October 1806, in consequence of too much exertion in the pursuit of studies that would have matured a mind which disease and poverty could not impair, and which Death itself destroyed rather than subdued. His poems abound in such beauties as must impress the reader with the liveliest regret that so short a period was allotted to talents, which would have dignified even the sacred functions he was destined to assume.

[H. K. White (1785-1806) published 'Clifton Grove' and other poems in 1803. Two volumes of his 'Remains,' consisting of poems, letters, etc., with a life by Southey, were issued in 1808. His tendency to epilepsy was increased by over-work at Cambridge. He once remarked to a friend that "were he to paint a picture of Fame, crowning a distinguished undergraduate after the Senate house examination, he would represent her as concealing a Death's head under a mask of Beauty" ('Life of H. K. W.', by Southey, i. 45). By "the soaring lyre, which else had sounded an immortal lay," Byron, perhaps, refers to the unfinished 'Christiad,' which, says Southey, "Henry had most at heart."]]

[Footnote 131: Lines 832-834, as they stand in the text, were inserted in MS. in both the Annotated Copies of the Fourth Edition.]]

[Footnote 132: "I consider Crabbe and Coleridge as the first of these times, in point of power and genius."—B., 1816.]

[Footnote 133: Mr. Shee, author of 'Rhymes on Art' and 'Elements of Art'. [Sir Martin Archer Shee (1770-1850) was President of the Royal Academy (1830-45). His 'Rhymes on Art' (1805) and 'Elements of Art' (1809), a poem in six cantos, will hardly be regarded as worthy of Byron's praise, which was probably quite genuine. He also wrote a novel, 'Harry Calverley', and other works.]]

[Footnote 134: Mr. Wright, late Consul-General for the Seven Islands, is author of a very beautiful poem, just published: it is entitled 'Horæ Ionicæ', and is descriptive of the isles and the adjacent coast of Greece. [Walter Rodwell Wright was afterwards President of the Court of Appeal in Malta, where he died in 1826. 'Horæ Ionicæ, a Poem descriptive of the Ionian Islands, and Part of the Adjacent Coast of Greece', was published in 1809. He is mentioned in one of Byron's long notes to 'Childe Harold', canto ii., dated Franciscan Convent, Mar. 17, 1811.]]

[Footnote 135: The translators of the Anthology have since published separate poems, which evince genius that only requires opportunity to attain eminence. [The Rev. Robert Bland (1779-1825) published, in 1806, 'Translations chiefly from the Greek Anthology, with Tales and Miscellaneous Poems'. In these he was assisted (see 'Life of the Rev. Francis Hodgson', vol. i. pp. 226-260) by Denman (afterwards Chief Justice), by Hodgson himself, and, above all, by John Herman Merivale (1779-1844), who subsequently, in 1813, was joint editor with him of 'Collections from the Greek Anthology', etc.]]

[Footnote 136: Erasmus Darwin (1731-1802), the grandfather of Charles Robert Darwin. Coleridge describes his poetry as "nothing but a succession of landscapes or paintings. It arrests the attention too often, and so prevents the rapidity necessary to pathos."—'Anima Poetæ', 1895, p. 5. His chief works are 'The Botanic Garden' (1789-92) and 'The Temple of Nature' (1803). Byron's censure of 'The Botanic Garden' is inconsistent with his principles, for Darwin's verse was strictly modelled on the lines of Pope and his followers. But the 'Loves of the Triangles' had laughed away the 'Loves of the Plants'.]]

[Footnote 137: The neglect of 'The Botanic Garden' is some proof of returning taste. The scenery is its sole recommendation.]

[Footnote 138: This was not Byron's mature opinion, nor had he so expressed himself in the review of Wordsworth's 'Poems' which he contributed to 'Crosby's Magazine' in 1807 ('Life', p. 669). His scorn was, in part, provoked by indignities offered to Pope and Dryden, and, in part, assumed because one Lake poet called up the rest; and it was good sport to flout and jibe at the "Fraternity." That the day would come when the message of Wordsworth would reach his ears and awaken his enthusiasm, he could not, of course, foresee (see 'Childe Harold', canto iii. stanzas 72, 'et seqq.').]]

[Footnote 139: Messrs. Lamb and Lloyd, the most ignoble followers of Southey and Co. [Charles Lloyd (1775-1839) resided for some months under Coleridge's roof, first in Bristol, and afterwards at Nether Stowey (1796-1797). He published, in 1796, a folio edition of his 'Poems on the Death of Priscilla Farmer', in which a sonnet by Coleridge and a poem of Lamb's were included. Lamb and Lloyd contributed several pieces to the second edition of Coleridge's Poems, published in 1797; and in 1798 they brought out a joint volume of their own composition, named 'Poems in Blank Verse'. 'Edmund Oliver', a novel, appeared also in 1798. An estrangement between Coleridge and Lloyd resulted in a quarrel with Lamb, and a drawing together of Lamb, Lloyd, and Southey. But Byron probably had in his mind nothing more than the lines in the 'Anti-Jacobin', where Lamb and Lloyd are classed with Coleridge and Southey as advocates of French socialism:—

"Coleridge and Southey, Lloyd and Lamb and Co.,
Tune all your mystic harps to praise Lepaux."

In later life Byron expressed a very different opinion of Lamb's literary merits. (See the preface to 'Werner', now first published.)]]

[Footnote 140: By the bye, I hope that in Mr. Scott's next poem, his hero or heroine will be less addicted to "Gramarye," and more to Grammar, than the Lady of the Lay and her Bravo, William of Deloraine.]

[Footnote 141: "Unjust."—B., 1816. [In 'Frost at Midnight', first published in 1798, Coleridge twice mentions his "Cradled infant."]]

[Footnote 142: The Rev. W. L. Bowles ('vide ante', p. 323, note 2), published, in 1789, 'Fourteen Sonnets written chiefly on Picturesque Spots during a Journey'.]]

[Footnote 143: It may be asked, why I have censured the Earl of CARLISLE, my guardian and relative, to whom I dedicated a volume of puerile poems a few years ago?—The guardianship was nominal, at least as far as I have been able to discover; the relationship I cannot help, and am very sorry for it; but as his Lordship seemed to forget it on a very essential occasion to me, I shall not burden my memory with the recollection. I do not think that personal differences sanction the unjust condemnation of a brother scribbler; but I see no reason why they should act as a preventive, when the author, noble or ignoble, has, for a series of years, beguiled a "discerning public" (as the advertisements have it) with divers reams of most orthodox, imperial nonsense. Besides, I do not step aside to vituperate the earl: no—his works come fairly in review with those of other Patrician Literati. If, before I escaped from my teens, I said anything in favour of his Lordship's paper books, it was in the way of dutiful dedication, and more from the advice of others than my own judgment, and I seize the first opportunity of pronouncing my sincere recantation. I have heard that some persons conceive me to be under obligations to Lord CARLISLE: if so, I shall be most particularly happy to learn what they are, and when conferred, that they may be duly appreciated and publicly acknowledged. What I have humbly advanced as an opinion on his printed things, I am prepared to support, if necessary, by quotations from Elegies, Eulogies, Odes, Episodes, and certain facetious and dainty tragedies bearing his name and mark:—

"What can ennoble knaves, or 'fools', or cowards?
Alas! not all the blood of all the Howards."

So says Pope. Amen!—"Much too savage, whatever the foundation might be."—B., 1816.]

[Footnote 144: Line 952. 'Note'—

"Tollere humo, victorque virum volitare per ora."

(VIRGIL.)]

[Footnote 145:

"The devil take that 'Phoenix'! How came it there?"

—B., 1816.]

[Footnote 146: The Rev. Charles James Hoare (1781-1865), a close friend of the leaders of the Evangelical party, gained the Seatonian Prize at Cambridge in 1807 with his poem on the 'Shipwreck of St. Paul'.]

[Footnote 147: Edmund Hoyle, the father of the modern game of whist, lived from 1672 to 1769. The Rev. Charles Hoyle, his "poetical namesake," was, like Hoare, a Seatonian prizeman, and wrote an epic in thirteen books on the 'Exodus'.]

[Footnote 148: The 'Games of Hoyle', well known to the votaries of Whist, Chess, etc., are not to be superseded by the vagaries of his poetical namesake ["illustrious Synonime" in 'MS.' and 'British Bards'], whose poem comprised, as expressly stated in the advertisement, all the "Plagues of Egypt."]

[Footnote 149: Here, as in line 391, "Fresh fish from Helicon," etc., Byron confounds Helicon and Hippocrene.]]

[Footnote 150: This person, who has lately betrayed the most rabid symptoms of confirmed authorship, is writer of a poem denominated 'The Art of Pleasing', as "Lucus a non lucendo," containing little pleasantry, and less poetry. He also acts as ["lies as" in 'MS.'] monthly stipendiary and collector of calumnies for the 'Satirist'. If this unfortunate young man would exchange the magazines for the mathematics, and endeavour to take a decent degree in his university, it might eventually prove more serviceable than his present salary.]

[Note.—An unfortunate young person of Emanuel College, Cambridge, ycleped Hewson Clarke, has lately manifested the most rabid symptoms of confirmed Authorship. His Disorder commenced some years ago, and the 'Newcastle Herald' teemed with his precocious essays, to the great edification of the Burgesses of Newcastle, Morpeth, and the parts adjacent even unto Berwick upon Tweed. These have since been abundantly scurrilous upon the [town] of Newcastle, his native spot, Mr. Mathias and Anacreon Moore. What these men had done to offend Mr. Hewson Clarke is not known, but surely the town in whose markets he had sold meat, and in whose weekly journal he had written prose deserved better treatment. Mr. H.C. should recollect the proverb "'tis a villainous bird that defiles his own nest." He now writes in the 'Satirist'. We recommend the young man to abandon the magazines for mathematics, and to believe that a high degree at Cambridge will be more advantageous, as well as profitable in the end, than his present precarious gleanings.]

[Hewson Clarke (1787-circ. 1832) was entered at Emmanuel Coll. Camb. circ. 1806 (see 'Postscript'). He had to leave the University without taking a degree, and migrated to London, where he devoted his not inconsiderable talents to contributions to the 'Satirist', the 'Scourge', etc. He also wrote: 'An Impartial History of the Naval, etc., Events of Europe ... from the French Revolution ... to the Conclusion of a General Peace' (1815); and a continuation of Hume's 'History of England', 2 vols. (1832).

The 'Satirist', a monthly magazine illustrated with coloured cartoons, was issued 1808-1814. 'Hours of Idleness' was reviewed Jan. 1808 (i. 77-81). "The Diary of a Cantab" (June, 1808, ii. 368) contains some verses of "Lord B——n to his Bear. To the tune of Lachin y gair." The last verse runs thus:—

"But when with the ardour of Love I am burning,
I feel for thy torments, I feel for thy care;
And weep for thy bondage, so truly discerning
What's felt by a 'Lord', may be felt by a 'Bear'."

In August, 1808 (iii. 78-86), there is a critique on 'Poems Original and Translated', in which the bear plays many parts. The writer "is without his bear and is himself muzzled," etc. Towards the close of the article a solemn sentence is passed on the author for his disregard of the advice of parents, tutors, friends; "but," adds the reviewer, "in the paltry volume before us we think we observe some proof that the still small voice of conscience will be heard in the cool of the day. Even now the gay, the gallant, the accomplished bear-leader is not happy," etc. Hence the castigation of "the sizar of Emmanuel College."]

[Footnote 151:

"Right enough: this was well deserved, and well laid on."

(B., 1816.)]

[Footnote 152:

"Into Cambridgeshire the Emperor Probus transported a considerable
body of Vandals."

(Gibbon's 'Decline and Fall', ii. 83.) There is no reason to doubt the truth of this assertion; the breed is still in high perfection.

We see no reason to doubt the truth of this statement, as a large stock of the same breed are to be found there at this day.—'British Bards'.

[Lines 981-984 do not occur in the 'MS'. Lines 981, 982, are inserted in
MS. in 'British Bards'.]]

[Footnote 153: This gentleman's name requires no praise: the man who [has surpassed Dryden and Gifford as a Translator.—'MS. British Bards'] in translation displays unquestionable genius may be well expected to excel in original composition, of which, it is to be hoped, we shall soon see a splendid specimen. [Francis Hodgson (1781-1852) was Byron's lifelong friend. His 'Juvenal' appeared in 1807; 'Lady Jane Grey and other Poems', in 1809; 'Sir Edgar, a Tale', in 1810. For other works and details, see 'Life of the Rev. Francis Hodgson', by the Rev. James T. Hodgson (1878).]]

[Footnote 154: Hewson Clarke, 'Esq'., as it is written.]

[Footnote 155: 'The Aboriginal Britons', an excellent ["most excellent" in 'MS.'] poem, by Richards. [The Rev. George Richards, D.D. (1769-1835), a Fellow of Oriel, and afterwards Rector of St. Martin's-in-the-Fields. 'The Aboriginal Britons', a prize poem, was published in 1792, and was followed by 'The Songs of the Aboriginal Bards of Britain' (1792), and various other prose and poetical works.]]

[Footnote: 156. With this verse the satire originally ended.]

[Footnote 157: A friend of mine being asked, why his Grace of Portland was likened to an old woman? replied, "he supposed it was because he was past bearing." (Even Homer was a punster—a solitary pun.)—['MS'.] His Grace is now gathered to his grandmothers, where he sleeps as sound as ever; but even his sleep was better than his colleagues' waking. 1811. [William Henry Cavendish, third Duke of Portland (1738-1809), Prime Minister in 1807, on the downfall of the Ministry of "All the Talents," till his death in 1809, was, as the wits said, "a convenient block to hang Whigs on," but was not, even in his vigour, a man of much intellectual capacity. When Byron meditated a tour to India in 1808, Portland declined to write on his behalf to the Directors of the East India Company, and couched his refusal in terms which Byron fancied to be offensive.]]

[Footnote 158: "Saw it August, 1809."—B., 1816. [The following notes were omitted from the Fifth Edition:—

"Calpe is the ancient name of Gibraltar. Saw it August, 1809.—B., 1816.

"Stamboul is the Turkish word for Constantinople. Was there the summer 1810."

To "Mount Caucasus," he adds, "Saw the distant ridge of,—1810, 1811"]]

[Footnote 159: Georgia.]

[Footnote 160: Mount Caucasus.]

[Footnote 161: Lord Elgin would fain persuade us that all the figures, with and without noses, in his stoneshop, are the work of Phidias! "Credat Judæus!" [R. Payne Knight, in his introduction to 'Specimens of Ancient Sculpture', published 1809, by the Dilettanti Society, throws a doubt on the Phidian workmanship of the "Elgin" marbles. See the Introduction to 'The Curse of Minerva'.]]

[Footnote 162: [Sir William Gell (1777-1836) published the 'Topography of Troy' (1804), the 'Geography and Antiquities of Ithaca' (1807), and the 'Itinerary of Greece' (1808). Byron reviewed the two last works in the 'Monthly Review' (August, 1811), ('Life', pp. 670, 676). Fresh from the scenes, he speaks with authority. "With Homer in his pocket and Gell on his sumpter-mule, the Odysseus tourist may now make a very classical and delightful excursion." The epithet in the original MS. was "coxcomb," but becoming acquainted with Gell while the satire was in the press, Byron changed it to "classic." In the fifth edition he altered it to "rapid," and appended this note:—"'Rapid,' indeed! He topographised and typographised King Priam's dominions in three days! I called him 'classic' before I saw the Troad, but since have learned better than to tack to his name what don't belong to it."]]

[Footnote 163: Mr. Gell's 'Topography of Troy and Ithaca' cannot fail to ensure the approbation of every man possessed of classical taste, as well for the information Mr. Gell conveys to the mind of the reader, as for the ability and research the respective works display.

"'Troy and Ithaca.' Visited both in 1810, 1811."—B., 1816.
"'Ithaca' passed first in 1809."—B., 1816.

"Since seeing the plain of Troy, my opinions are somewhat changed as to the above note. Gell's survey was hasty and superficial."—B., 1816.]

[Footnote 164:

"Singular enough, and 'din' enough, God knows."

(B., 1816).]

[Footnote 165:

"The greater part of this satire I most sincerely wish had never been written-not only on account of the injustice of much of the critical, and some of the personal part of it—but the tone and temper are such as I cannot approve."

BYRON. July 14, 1816. 'Diodati, Geneva'.]

[Footnote i:

'Truth be my theme, and Censure guide my song.'

['MS. M.']

[Footnote ii:

'But thou, at least, mine own especial quill
Dipt in the dew drops from Parnassus' hill,
Shalt ever honoured and regarded be,
By more beside no doubt, yet still by me.'

['MS. M.']]

[Footnote iii:

'And men through life her willing slaves obey.'

['MS. Second, Third, and Fourth Editions.']]

[Footnote iv:

'Unfolds her motley store to suit the time.'—

['MS. Second, Third, and Fourth Editions.']]

[Footnote v:

'When Justice halts and Right begins to fail.'

['MS. Second, Third, and Fourth Editions.']]

[Footnote vi:

'A mortal weapon'.

['MS. M.']

[Footnote vii:

   'Yet Titles sounding lineage cannot save
Or scrawl or scribbler from an equal grave,
Lamb had his farce but that Patrician name
Failed to preserve the spurious brat from shame.'

['MS.']]

[Footnote viii: 'a lucky hit.'

['Second, Third, and Fourth Editions.']]

[Footnote ix: 'No dearth of rhyme.'

['British Bards'.]]

[Footnote x: 'The Press oppressed.'

['British Bards'.]]

[Footnote xi:

'While Southey's Epics load.'

['British Bards'.]]

[Footnote xii: 'O'er taste awhile these Infidels prevail.'

['MS.']]

[Footnote xiii:

'Erect and hail an idol of their own.'

['MS.']]

[Footnote xiv:

'Not quite a footpad———.'

['British Bards'.]]

[Footnote xv: 'Low may they sink to merited contempt.'

['British Bards'.]]

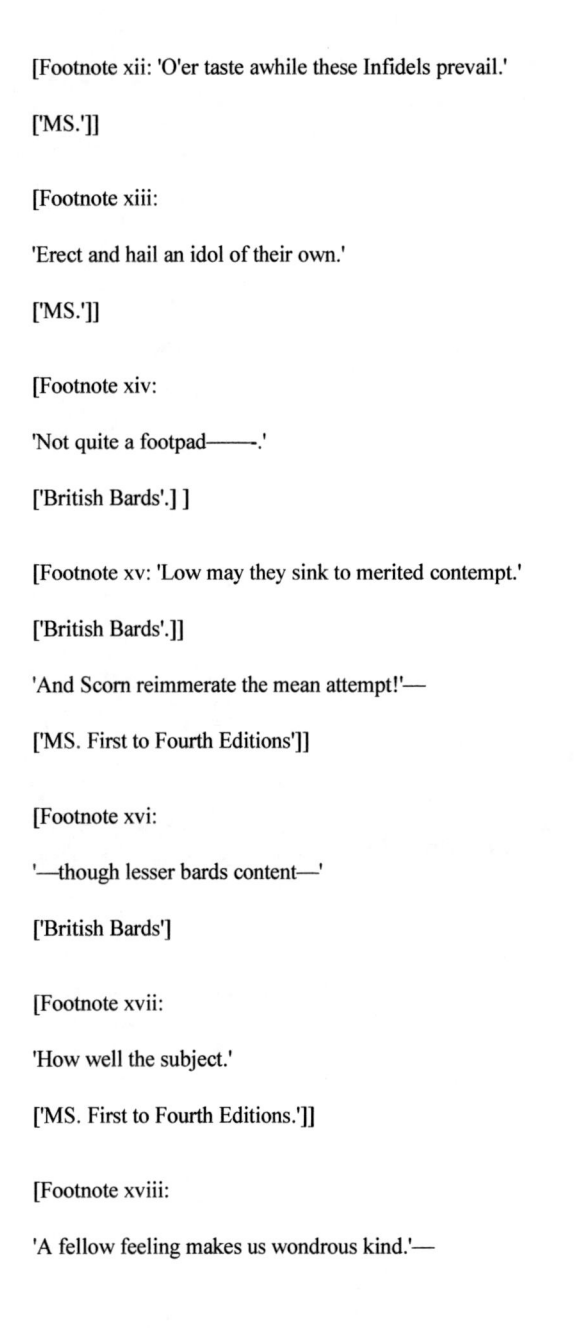

'And Scorn reimmerate the mean attempt!'—

['MS. First to Fourth Editions']]

[Footnote xvi:

'—though lesser bards content—'

['British Bards']

[Footnote xvii:

'How well the subject.'

['MS. First to Fourth Editions.']]

[Footnote xviii:

'A fellow feeling makes us wondrous kind.'—

['British Bards, First to Fourth Editions.']]

[Footnote xix:

'Who fain would'st.'

['British Bards, First to Fifth Editions'.]]

[Footnote xx:

'Mend thy life, and sin no more.'

['MS.']]

[Footnote xxi:

'And o'er harmonious nonsense.'

['MS. First Edition.']]

[Footnote xxii:

'In many marble-covered volumes view
Hayley, in vain attempting something new,
Whether he spin his comedies in rhyme,
Or scrawls as Wood and Barclay [A] walk, 'gainst Time.'

['MS. British Bards', and 'First to Fourth Editions.']

[Sub-Footnote A: Captain Robert Barclay (1779-1854) of Ury, agriculturalist and pedestrian, came of a family noted for physical strength and endurance. Byron saw him win his walk against Wood at Newmarket. (See Angelo's 'Reminiscences' (1837), vol. ii. pp. 37-44.) In July, 1809, Barclay completed his task of walking a thousand miles in a thousand hours, at the rate of one mile in each and every hour. (See, too, for an account of Barclay, 'The Eccentric Review' (1812), i. 133-150.)]]

[Footnote xxiii:

'Breaks into mawkish lines each holy Book'.

['MS. First Edition'.]]

[Footnote xxiv:

'Thy "Sympathy" that'.

['British Bards'.]]

[Footnote xxv:

  'And shows dissolved in sympathetic tears'.
'——in thine own melting tears.—'

['MS. First to Fourth Editions'.]]

[Footnote xxvi:

  'Whether in sighing winds them seek'st relief
Or Consolation in a yellow leaf.—'

['MS. first to Fourth Editions.']]

[Footnote xxvii:

'What pretty sounds.'

['British Bards.']]

[Footnote xxviii:

'Thou fain woulds't——'

['British Bards.']]

[Footnote xxix:

'But to soft themes'.

['British Bards, First Edition'.]]

[Footnote xxx:

'The Bard has wove'.

['British Bards'.]]

[Footnote xxxi:

  'If Pope, since mortal, not untaught to err
Again demand a dull biographer'.

['MS'.]]

[Footnote xxxii:

  'Too much in Turtle Bristol's sons delight
Too much in Bowls of Rack prolong the night.—'

['MS. Second to Fourth Editions'.]

'Too much o'er Bowls.'

['Second and Third Editions'.]]

[Footnote xxxiii:

'And yet why'.

['British Bards'.]]

[Footnote xxxiv:

'Or old or young'.

['British Bards'.]]

[Footnote xxxv:

—'yes, I'm sure all may.'

['Quarto Proof Sheet']

[Footnote xxxvi:

  'While Cloacina's holy pontiff Lambe [3]
As he himself was damned shall try to damn'.

['British Bards'.]

[Sub-Footnote A. We have heard of persons who "when the Bagpipe sings in the nose cannot contain their urine for affection," but Mr. L. carries it a step further than Shakespeare's diuretic amateurs, being notorious at school and college for his inability to contain—anything. We do not know to what "Pipe" to attribute this additional effect, but the fact is uncontrovertible.—['Note' to Quarto Proof bound up with 'British Bards'.]]

[Footnote xxxvii:

'Lo! long beneath'—.

['British Bards'.]]

[Footnote xxxviii:

 'And grateful to the founder of the feast
Declare his landlord can translate at least'.—

['MS. British Bards. First to Fourth Editions'.]]

[Footnote xxxix:

'—are fed because they write.'

['British Bards'.]]

[Footnote xl:

'Princes in Barrels, Counts in arbours pent.—

[MS. British Bards'.]]

[Footnote xli:

'His "damme, poohs."'

['MS. First Edition.']]

[Footnote xlii:

  'While Kenny's World just suffered to proceed
Proclaims the audience very kind indeed'.—

['MS. British Bards. First to Fourth Editions'.]]

[Footnote xliii:

'Resume her throne again'.—

['MS. British Bards. First to Fourth Editions.']]

[Footnote xliv:—

'and Kemble lives to tread'.—

['British Bards. First to Fourth Editions.']]

[Footnote xlv:

'St. George [A] and Goody Goose divide the prize.'—

[MS. alternative in British Bards.]

  [Sub-Footnote A: We need not inform the reader that we do not allude to the Champion of England who slew the Dragon. Our St. George is content to draw status with a very different kind of animal.—[Pencil note to 'British Bards'.]]]

[Footnote xlvi:

'Its humble flight to splendid Pantomimes'.

['British Bards. MS']]

[Footnote xlvii:

'Behold the new Petronius of the times
The skilful Arbiter of modern crimes.'

['MS.']

[Footnote xlviii:

'——a Paget for your wife.'

['MS. First to Fourth Editions.']]

[Footnote xlix:

'From Grosvenor Place or Square'.

['MS. British Bards'.]]

[Footnote l:

'On one alone Apollo deigns to smile
And crowns a new Roscommon in Carlisle.'

['MS. Addition to British Bards.']

'Nor e'en a hackneyed Muse will deign to smile
On minor Byron, or mature Carlisle.'

[First Edition.]

[Footnote li:

'Yet at their fiat——'
'Yet at their nausea——.'

['MS. Addition to British Bards'.]]

[Footnote lii:

'Such sneering fame.'

['British Bards']

[Footnote liii:

  'Though Bell has lost his nightingales and owls,
Matilda snivels still and Hafiz howls,
And Crusca's spirit rising from the dead
Revives in Laura, Quiz, and X. Y. Z.'—

['British Bards. First to Third Editions', 1810.]]

[Footnote liv:

'None since the past have claimed the tribute due'.

['British Bards. MS'.]]

[Footnote lv:

  'From Albion's cliffs to Caledonia's coast.
Some few who know to write as well as feel'.

['MS'.]]

[Footnote lvi:

  'The spoiler came; and all thy promise fair
Has sought the grave, to sleep for ever there.—'

['First to Fourth Editions']]

[Footnote lvii:

'On him may meritorious honours tend
While doubly mingling,'.

['MS. erased'.]]

Footnote lviii:

'And you united Bards'.

['MS. Addition to British Bards'.]

'And you ye nameless'.

['MS. erased'.]]

[Footnote lvix:

'Translation's servile work at length disown
And quit Achaia's Muse to court your own'.

['MS. Addition to British Bards'.]]

[Footnote lx:

'Let these arise and anxious of applause'.

['British Bards. MS'.]]

[Footnote lxi:

'But not in heavy'.

['British Bards. MS'.]]

[Footnote lxii:

'Let prurient Southey cease'.

['MS. British Bards'.]]

[Footnote lxiii:

'still the babe at nurse'.

['MS'.]

'Let Lewis jilt our nurseries with alarm
With tales that oft disgust and never charm'.

[Footnote lxiv:

'But thou with powers—'

['MS. British Bards'.]]

[Footnote lxv:

'Let MOORE be lewd; let STRANGFORD steal from MOORE'.

['MS. First to Fourth Editions'.]]

[Footnote lxvi:

'For outlawed Sherwood's tales.'

['MS. Brit. Bards. Eds.' 1-4.]

[Footnote lxvii:

'And even spurns the great Seatonian prize.—'

['MS. First to Fourth Editions' (a correction in the Annotated Copy).]]

[Footnote lxviii:

'With odes by Smyth [A] and epic songs by Hoyle,
Hoyle whose learn'd page, if still upheld by whist
Required no sacred theme to bid us list.—'

['MS. British Bards.']

[Sub-Footnote A: William Smyth (1766-1849). Professor of Modern History at Cambridge, published his 'English Lyrics' (in 1806), and several other works.]

[Footnote lxix:

'Yet hold—as when by Heaven's supreme behest,
If found, ten righteous had preserved the Rest
In Sodom's fated town—for Granta's name
Let Hodgson's Genius plead and save her fame
But where fair Isis, etc.'

['MS.' and 'British Bards.']]

[Footnote lxx:

'See Clarke still striving piteously to please
Forgets that Doggrel leads not to degrees.—'

['MS. Fragment' bound up with 'British Bards'.]

[Footnote lxxi:

'So sunk in dullness and so lost in shame
That Smythe and Hodgson scarce redeem thy fame.—'

['MS. Addition to British Bards. First to Fourth Editions'.]]

[Footnote lxxii:

'——is wove.—'

[MS. British Bards' and 'First to Fourth Editions'.]]

[Footnote lxxiii:

'And modern Britons justly praise their sires.'—

['MS. British Bards' and 'First to Fourth Editions]]

[Footnote lxxiv:

'—what her sons must know too well.'

['British Bards]]

[Footnote lxxv:

  'Zeal for her honour no malignant Rage,
Has bade me spurn the follies of the age.—'

['MS. British Bards'. First Edition]]

[Footnote lxxvi:

'—Ocean's lonely Queen.'

['British Bards']]

'—Ocean's mighty Queen.'

['First to Fourth Editions']]

[Footnote: lxxvii.

  'Like these thy cliffs may sink in ruin hurled
The last white ramparts of a falling world'.—

['British Bards MS.']]

[Footnote: lxxviii.

'But should I back return, no lettered rage
Shall drag my common-place book on the stage:
Let vain Valentia [A] rival luckless Carr,
And equal him whose work he sought to mar.—'

['Second to Fourth Editions'.]

[Sub-Footnote: A. Lord Valentia (whose tremendous travels are forthcoming with due decorations, graphical, topographical, typographical) deposed, on Sir John Carr's unlucky suit, that Mr. Dubois's satire prevented his purchase of 'The Stranger' in Ireland.—Oh, fie, my lord! has your lordship no more feeling for a fellow-tourist?—but "two of a trade," they say, etc. [George Annesley, Viscount Valentia (1769-1844), published, in 1809, 'Voyages and Travels to India, Ceylon, the Red Sea, Abyssinia, and Egypt in the Years 1802-6'. Byron calls him "vain" Valentia, because his "accounts of ceremonies attending his lordship's interviews with several of the petty princes" suggest the thought "that his principal errand to India was to measure certain rank in the British peerage against the gradations of Asiatic royalty."—'Eclectic Review', August, 1809. In August, 1808, Sir John Carr, author of numerous 'Travels', brought an unsuccessful action for damages against Messrs. Hood and Sharpe, the publishers of the parody of his works by Edward Dubois,—'My Pocket Book: or Hints for a Ryghte Merrie and Conceitede Tour, in 4to, to be called "The Stranger in Ireland in 1805,"' By a Knight Errant, and dedicated to the papermakers. (See Letter to Hodgson, August 6, 1809, and suppressed stanza (stanza lxxxvii.) of the first canto of 'Childe Harold'.)]]

[Footnote lxxix:

'To stun mankind, with Poesy or Prose'.

['Second to Fourth Editions'.]

[Footnote lxxx: 'Thus much I've dared to do, how far my lay'.—

['First to Fourth Editions'.]]

POSTSCRIPT TO THE SECOND EDITION.

I have been informed, since the present edition went to the press, that my trusty and well-beloved cousins, the Edinburgh Reviewers, are preparing a most vehement critique on my poor, gentle, 'unresisting' Muse, whom they have already so be-deviled with their ungodly ribaldry;

"Tantæne animis coelestibus Iræ!"

I suppose I must say of JEFFREY as Sir ANDREW AGUECHEEK saith, "an I had known he was so cunning of fence, I had seen him damned ere I had fought him." What a pity it is that I shall be beyond the Bosphorus before the next number has passed the Tweed! But I yet hope to light my pipe with it in Persia. [1]

My Northern friends have accused me, with justice, of personality towards their great literary Anthropophagus, Jeffery; but what else was to be done with him and his dirty pack, who feed by "lying and slandering," and slake their thirst by "evil speaking"? I have adduced facts already well known, and of JEFFREY's mind I have stated my free opinion, nor has he thence sustained any injury:—what scavenger was ever soiled by being pelted with mud? It may be said that I quit England because I have censured there "persons of honour and wit about town;" but I am coming back again, and their vengeance will keep hot till my return. Those who know me can testify that my motives for leaving England are very different from fears, literary or personal: those who do not, may one day be convinced. Since the publication of this thing, my name has not been concealed; I have been mostly in London, ready to answer for my transgressions, and in daily expectation of sundry cartels; but, alas! "the age of chivalry is over," or, in the vulgar tongue, there is no spirit now-a-days.

There is a youth ycleped Hewson Clarke (subaudi 'esquire'), a sizer of Emanuel College, and, I believe, a denizen of Berwick-upon-Tweed, whom I have introduced in these pages to much better company than he has been accustomed to meet; he is, notwithstanding, a very sad dog, and for no reason that I can discover, except a personal quarrel with a bear, kept by me at Cambridge to sit for a fellowship, and whom the jealousy of his Trinity contemporaries prevented from success, has been abusing me, and, what is worse, the defenceless innocent above mentioned, in the 'Satirist' for one year and some months. I am utterly unconscious of having given him any provocation; indeed, I am guiltless of having heard his name, till coupled with the 'Satirist'. He has therefore no reason to complain, and I dare say that, like Sir Fretful Plagiary, he is rather 'pleased' than otherwise. I have now mentioned all who have done me the honour to notice me and mine, that is, my bear and my book, except the editor of the 'Satirist', who, it seems, is a gentleman—God wot! I wish he could impart a little of his gentility to his subordinate scribblers. I hear that Mr. JERNINGHAM[1] is about to take up the cudgels for his Mæcenas, Lord Carlisle. I hope not: he was one of the few, who, in the very short intercourse I had with him, treated me with kindness when a boy; and whatever he may say or do, "pour on, I will endure." I have nothing further to add, save a general note of thanksgiving to readers, purchasers, and publishers, and, in the words of SCOTT, I wish

"To all and each a fair good night,
And rosy dreams and slumbers light."

[Footnote 1: The article never appeared, and Lord Byron, in the 'Hints from Horace', taunted Jeffrey with a silence which seemed to indicate that the critic was beaten from the field.]

[Footnote 2: Edward Jerningham (1727-1812), third son of Sir George Jerningham, Bart., was an indefatigable versifier. Between the publication of his first poem, 'The Nunnery', in 1766, and his last, 'The Old Bard's Farewell', in 1812, he sent to the press no less than thirty separate compositions. As a contributor to the 'British Album', Gifford handled him roughly in the 'Baviad' (lines 21, 22); and Mathias, in a note to 'Pursuits of Literature', brackets him with Payne Knight as "ecrivain du commun et poëte vulgaire." He was a dandy with a literary turn, who throughout a long life knew every one who was worth knowing. Some of his letters have recently been published (see 'Jerningham Letters', two vols., 1896).]